T5-AFS-480

COPY 1

Sex Is RED

Sex Is RED

Bill Gaston

CORMORANT
BOOKS

The publisher gratefully acknowledges the support of the Canada Council for the Arts and the Ontario Arts Council for its publishing program. The publisher also acknowledges the financial support of the Government of Canada through the Book Publishing Industry Development Program for its publishing activities.

The following stories from the collection have been published previously: "Saving Eve's Father" and "Angels Kill Hummingbirds" in *The Malahat Review;* "Sex Is Red" (appeared as "Painting the Dishes Red"), "Dug", and "With Your Hand in Satan's Gleaming Guts" in *Exile;* "Your First Time" (appeared as "My First Time") and "The Divine Right of Kings" in *The New Quarterly;* "The Sunday Lise Saw Jesus" in *Capilano Review;* "Fire Heaven" in *The Fiddlehead.*

Cover Design by Bill Douglas @ The Bang

Printed and bound in Canada.

APR   8 1999   Cormorant Books Inc.
RR 1
Dunvegan, Ontario
K0C 1J0

Canadian Cataloguing in Publication Data
Gaston, Bill 1953-
Sex is red
ISBN 1-896951-09-0
I. Title.
PS8563.A76S39 1998 C813'.54 C98-900964-5
PR9199.3.G37S39 1998

For Lily Victoria

CONTENTS

SAVING EVE'S FATHER

PEOPLE SAID YOU COULD BUILD another general store in Burkitts and as long as it had a video gambling machine in it, it would send the owner to Florida every March or April, cabin-fever season. At Lyle Green's— the government let him have just the one machine—all day there was a lineup waiting for the chance to put a paycheque into it, or a pension into it, or last-will-and-testament money into it, whatever. As Alex's aunt said, you could hardly see through the cigarette smoke to find yourself to the loafs of bread.

Maybe Eve's father had bad cabin fever, maybe it was that. It was through his aunt that Alex heard about what he had done to Eve. Eve was Alex's girlfriend, though what exactly was meant by this wasn't clear yet. Eve had announced the word to him last week when they parked at the edge of the lake ice and had their thermos of tea together. After this word came some long kissing, and bubbling smiles, and a new shyness on her part, but nothing else, not yet. In any case it made Alex happier than he'd been in a while, probably since his parents went through the ice, four years ago now. He'd had a silent crush on Eve Gartner for years, and he could hardly believe this was happening. When they kissed, his stomach fell right to his feet and it was almost too much.

His aunt had a way of delivering big news. She would always turn her back to say it, and put away dishes or neaten things up. She'd told Alex about his parents this way, putting her good cups on the top shelf with her back turned, words coming out very clear and plain. By the time she said he could come live with her if he wanted, she was onto the plates. Today, she turned her back and folded napkins to tell him about Eve.

"Eve's father hit her today in Lyle Green's."

"What?"

"Eve's father hit her today in Lyle Green's."

"Why?"

"She was only doing him a favour, and if I'd been any one of those half-dozen who saw it, Mike Gartner would be in jail tonight."

"Why'd Mr. Gartner do it?"

"Eve was trying to pry him away from that machine home to eat. I'm surprised he took a hand off the buttons long enough to hit her."

Alex was already half into his coat. His aunt turned to look at him and her face spoke plainly, asking him if he was sure he wanted to get mixed up with that family.

He knew he had no choice in the matter of getting mixed up with her family, and it wasn't like Eve had had any choice to begin with either. But the Gartners were okay really, even Mr., though smiling wasn't easy for him and he didn't like stringing lots of words together. It was odd that he had the hockey player's name, especially since the other Mike Gartner had been in the news a lot with the goal-scoring milestones and being traded to Toronto. Alex always called Eve's father Mr. Gartner.

As far as Alex knew, he had never hit Eve before. Eve had never given any hint of it at least, and she seemed to like her dad in the normal way. Losing his job when the base closed had been tough, but no tougher than on anyone else. And though Eve had once mentioned how her mother was mad at her dad for wasting money on that machine, it didn't seem like a crisis or anything, not like with some others, like Mrs. Pollock and what appeared to be an out-and-out addiction where you're talking a gambled old-age cheque and no food for two weeks, except maybe—so the rumour went—cat food.

It was snowing big wet flakes under the streetlight, as pretty as the first snowfall of the year, though tonight everyone would be hoping this was the year's last. Alex knocked and got Eve to come out. They went around the corner and she walked into his arms and told him and cried about it, and though it was an awful story it felt good to Alex to be able to hold her through her storm.

She said she'd gone to the store and her father was up there on the stool, playing, and she'd told him in a whisper that lunch was on the table and Mum was getting mad, and please come. He'd told her he'd damn well waited all morning to get a turn, he'd be a while, stick the damn lunch in the oven why don't you, and Eve could tell he was losing money and also embarrassed at having to explain himself in front of his friends. She'd said "please come" again, and when he didn't answer she said it again louder, and now it was clear to everyone that she wasn't talking about just lunch. Then Eve made the mistake of getting mad, and yelling at him about her money.

"Your money?" Alex whispered into her neck. He could smell the shampoo she used, and also her parents' smoke.

"He borrowed a hundred dollars last week and blew it in a day and hasn't paid me back. I yelled at him that I wasn't going to lend him any more money. Then he hit me with the back of his hand. Look."

Eve showed him the tiny scrape from his ring on the side of her nose. Then pressing her palm to it as if to staunch something flowing out, she began to cry harder.

"Holy jeez." Alex could see it clearly—Mr. Gartner startled, a grunt and a swing of his arm, his face with no expression on it.

"I didn't know he was blowing money like that."

"Mum's really worried."

"I can see how she would be."

"And next year's all.... It's not just the hundred. I've had to pay some bills and stuff."

"Your school money?"

Eve nodded and looked off into the falling snow. For over a year she'd been putting in whatever hours she could as a janitor at both the old folks' and the post office, saving to go to university. "I guess it can turn into a disease with some people," Eve said, looking philosophical, staring through the thick flakes.

"That's sure what you read."

"They don't blink. He looks like a pigeon hitting those buttons. I wish somebody'd put a fucking brick through it."

The next day Alex took his snowmobile for a last spin over the lake. He stopped out in the middle and took off his helmet and tilted his face up and felt how warm the sun was getting. The surface ice was tacky. A few years back, when he first took to stopping and resting way out here in the middle, where in each direction the land was just a dark band on the horizon and you could see only the forest but not the trees—so went the joke—he knew that people thought he was communing with his parents. Maybe the first time he'd stopped way out here he'd been trying for something like that. But then when he learned that communion with them had nothing to do with where he was or wasn't, his stopping had only to do with loving the shock of the contrast, of switching from the full-throttle roaring screaming rush to the complete stillness of stopping out here. And listening to absolute nothing, feeling like an ant in the middle of a vast white field. Then climbing back on for the roaring rush to shore.

He sat ass-backwards and reclined with his head on the handlebars. The spring sun felt like—a woman's love. People with bad cabin fever should spend more time out here, get the sky over them, get out of their hot little houses. He should invite Mr. Gartner fishing after breakup, before the tourists started coming and taking up Alex's time. His name was getting around, mostly lawyers from Boston and Hartford who had never caught a salmon. It should be a good year again, with the dollar still falling. For American fishermen it was like holidaying in the Third World now.

What else could he do for Mr. Gartner? That is, what could he do for Eve? He was ashamed of himself for reacting as he had, for feeling a secret horny joy on realizing Eve might not have the money to be going off to school after all. He had instantly offered to help her, though she knew as well as he did that he had three hundred and fifteen in the bank and that next year at this time he would likely have around the same.

He lay back anyway and envisioned a rich season of millionaires' tips, where he could hand her a wad at the end of August and send her to school, a double sacrifice that would get him Eve's lifelong respect. He also envisioned an Eve stuck here, bitter, living through an awful family time and smiling even less than her father.

After his horny joy had come guilt, and he'd promised her he'd do something. He'd seen the quick, hopeful flash in her eye, but then she couldn't help but see him as the fool he felt like.

The next morning Alex was at the bank door when it opened. He withdrew three hundred fourteen, leaving the one buck in to keep the account alive. He felt silly with the old felt whisky bag that he used to carry marbles in. Now it was full of loonies and the strings were threatening to break from the weight, but didn't it look just like a pirate's pouch of gold?

Even with his marble bag, and day pack over his shoulder, no one noticed him in Lyle Green's. The dim and purgatorial store (Green used forty-watt bulbs people said) was already smoky from the men around the machine. Eve's father was one of them, though it was bald Mr. Tate up on the stool.

Alex lurked by the fishing gear, dusty stuff that hadn't moved in years. No one addressed him as he watched out of the corner of his eye. He would pick his spot and be aggressive. He knew that being seen by these particular men would likely get him called "Ed," after the shy young native in Northern Exposure. When the show first came out, friends decided Alex's manner was just like Ed's, especially the way he'd hang his head and nod and agree. So the name stuck. These men here would call him Ed and not even know why.

Alex moved to magazines and dared Lyle Green's scowl by reading one, about current Hollywood movies and all the inside things the stars and directors were saying. Flipping past a spread on Jane Campion, Alex remembered Ed's thing for Hollywood movies, and he put the magazine down.

Mr. Tate said in singsong, "Enough's enough," and lifted his birdlike hands in a shrug. His legs looked too skinny to bear weight and he sometimes wore an ascot and was otherwise a strange man for around here. He got down off the stool and Alex moved in. The lineup was informal from the looks of it and no one was being pushy. Or maybe the others were broke, maybe they were watchers today. Whatever the case, Alex nudged between Eve's father and Roman Burkitts, climbed the stool, said, "Here we go," and thunked his pirate's bag down on the counter beside the over-spilling ashtray.

"It's Ed! Hey Eddie!" Mr. Tate sounded like he might have won a few dollars.

"Hi," Alex said without turning.

"Hey, it was my turn," said Roman Burkitts, hulking in his greasy jeanjacket, but he was smiling.

"Gotta be quicker'n that," Alex smiled back, and so far everything was allowable and friendly, though Eve's father hadn't spoken.

Alex had about a dozen overflow loonies in his shirt pocket. He pulled one out, put it into the slot, heard it tinkle and chunk, and the machine was reborn with a shuffle of eager, face-up cards. He'd played once before, months ago on a whim, losing four quarters in about two minutes. He would have lost them faster had he known which buttons to push.

This dollar lasted three minutes. Two wins upped it to two-fifty before he lost six games straight. He reached into his pocket and slid five loonies into the machine, twenty credits.

"Now we're talkin'," grunted Burkitts, with a lust in his voice almost as if he were the one playing.

It took Alex twenty minutes to lose his shirt-pocket money. When he propped up his marble bag, untied it, and lifted a few dollars off the top, Mr. Tate almost shouted.

"Holy shit, boy, that full of money?"

Alex slid ten into the slot. He took his water bottle from his day pack and set it beside the money bag. He wiggled his ass on the hard stool to get settled, and otherwise let his focused demeanour answer Mr. Tate's question.

Eve's father had apparently put two and two together. His voice was a smoker's gravelly whisper, one that caught in his throat and tripped the words like a growing boy's voice breaking, and this would embarrass a man like him. "What you, what you trying to do, Alex?"

Alex pressed *Deal*. He hadn't had to put words to this yet. "I don't know. Maybe trying to save you all some money." Alex said it with some respect, and likely they thought he was only being funny, but his bravery to say it at all sat him up straight.

The first two hours there were complaints about wanting a turn at the machine, but most were joking because it was still a case of Alex being a novelty. He attracted a good-sized audience and lots of opinions about how to play draw poker. Mr. Tate had a head for percentages. Alex was offered cigarettes, because gamblers smoked. Most assumed he was here to make a pile, had come prepared to go for broke, and they saw nothing strange in that.

By the fourth hour many spectators had left and come back, and more than one wanted to play and said so. Their movements were stiff and jerky, and though they caged their demand in a joke, as in, "Yuz had time to win TWO million, give someone else a crack boy," it was plain they were itchy and getting pissed off. Alex, not turning away from the screen, said only, "Not finished yet," and he had to say it more than once. Some complained to Lyle Green behind the counter and the owner came over—clearly hating to leave the till, but happy up to now because of the extra coffee and subs and whatnot he was selling—and asked Alex if he planned on playing for ever. Alex's steady nodding started a grumbling among them. Then when they saw with their own eyes Alex take the big jar from his day pack, excuse himself to the three ladies, pivot away from them on the stool and use the jar for a goddamn pisspot, some of them held a meeting outside. Head down, winning a bit and losing a bit more, Alex heard laughter out there, but he heard angry shouts too.

At three-thirty, over five hours into his game, Eve came in. Her face said she knew. Her father had left a while back and hadn't returned. Eve joined the ring of people and stood there like the rest. She watched silently for a few minutes. When she said, "Alex?" the ring disbanded as the others moved off to give the two some room. Maybe it was something in her voice, or maybe it was the nature of towns this size that they know who's with who almost before the couple know it themselves.

Eve came up, leaned an arm on the top of the machine and hunched down to watch the screen and its unfolding game, her head side by side with his. She spoke softly. "You down much?"

Alex glanced at the marble bag, appraising its collapsed top. "I dunno. Fifty or sixty. Maybe seventy." He made a joke. "Maybe seventy-one."

"So, I mean, what is it," Eve began to ask, slowly, her tone that of someone who has realized she doesn't know another as well as she thought, "what is it you're doing?"

At first Alex just laughed softly, and glanced up at her. He tried to explain with his eyes. When she didn't smile back, he thought about what words he should use for something he wasn't clear on, himself. "Well, I'm not exactly sure," he said. "Couple of things, maybe." He smiled again. "If I win a lot, you won't have to worry about school." Afraid she might think he meant he'd be so rich she wouldn't have to go to school at all, he added, "Won't have to worry about tuition."

"You're not going to win a lot."

"No. Probably not." He paused. "The other thing, then, the main thing, was that as long as I'm playing, they're not."

Eve hesitated a moment before saying, "You mean, he's not."

"Right. I guess that's it."

Eve was so still beside him it felt like she wasn't breathing. Alex found himself wishing she would touch him, just a friendly something on the shoulder, but instead it felt as if everything about him, even the way he was pushing the buttons, was being studied. "This thing," Eve said in a whisper, "isn't very logical." Alex shook his head, no, in agreement, pressed buttons to keep the two sixes and draw three, and laughed, because what else could he do? He hit again. No third six came up, he lost another dollar, and Eve was gone without a word. Now Alex felt groundless, and haunted by the scraping of boots as people edged back in around him.

The bananas and chicken thigh he'd brought from home he'd eaten too early and he was very hungry. He guessed from the dying light out the window that it must be evening. He hadn't asked the time for hours because he'd decided that his moneybag was all that mattered and it was like the sand in an hourglass in any case. Plus people wouldn't tell him the time any more, or they lied. When he asked if someone would please buy him a sub, Roman Burkitts said to get up and get it yourself.

There were those who came and went and came back, smiling and shaking their heads at the show, a large part of which was the glaring group of watchers who wanted to play and whose humour was long gone, unless you counted the kind that tries to stab you in the side.

"I guess his skidoo runs on fuckin' syrup," Mr. Tate said a foot from Alex's ear, referring to Alex's snowmobile which was parked outside, "because the boys have been pourin' sugar in his tank all fuckin' day." Mr. Tate's hard talk didn't go with his ascot or his thinness, and it made Alex queasy.

Alex was on a particularly long losing streak, and had maybe a hundred left. Earlier in the day he'd tried delaying tactics: yawns and stretches, and elaborate ponderings of what cards to save and how much to bet, and once even fingering through a scatter of loonies on the counter, asking aloud which was the lucky one, jeez, which one should I use to change my luck? At this, two men threatened to drag him bodily off the stool, and Alex knew they would have done it because now they were feeling mocked. From then on he'd played at a reasonable pace. But he was losing quickly and steadily.

He'd noticed some patterns to the machine. It was supposed to be random in its dealing of cards, but there's no way you should get a full house, a flush, a few two-pair games, and finally a three of a kind, all in a row, and then not get even a better-than-jacks pair for twenty-odd games straight. Was it programmed to do that? To suck you in with quick wins and riches, then drain you slowly but surely, hoping it had all your money by the time it took giddiness to fall to just hope, then to impatience, then anger, then finally to the embarrassed sweats and the panic. Or did luck turn off and on like that, like something you could feel as clearly as the hot or cold spray of a shower?

Alex was weak-hungry and, nailed to the stool, his body had run out of positions it could relax in. He had to squirm his way out of an ache every minute or so. Sometimes, sliding money into the slot, he caught himself wanting the coins to disappear faster so it would be over. But then he'd hit. A third king would come, its face looking better than money itself, and the pealing angel-song of electronic bells would fix the world for a second, as credits on the screen clicked up, up, up, and some feeling deep and good would sit him straighter again, and he'd watch the screen more carefully for a game or two—that bright, bright cartoon-blue screen, an eager blue that got inside you more than you got inside it, a blue that felt like some version of paradise.

Eve's father had come and gone a few times and hadn't said a word. They'd met eyes once, and Alex had seen a mix of things there, difficult to read. But it was getting hard for Alex to see anything other than the screen. The sun had fallen, the windows were black, and Lyle Green's forty watts couldn't compete. Alex's vision was beginning to cross and blur. To stretch his eyes he looked up into the store but could make out little except the glints off potato-chip bags, or the general shadow of an aisle, or the vague human shapes watching his screen from a distance, the red tips of their smokes after the sulphurous flaring of a match.

At one-thirty a.m. his money was so low that after he hefted his bag to test it, it jingled rather than thunked when he set it down. Maybe twenty, maybe fifteen dollars. Alex was head-swimming tired, and he couldn't hide it, and the people still there were impatient to end it too but they couldn't leave until it was over. Lyle Green said, "I'll be closin' up soon boys," which was a nice way of excusing Alex for the loss, taking the spotlight off him. It was understood Lyle Green would stay open for as long as it took.

Another loss, another. Roman Burkitts suggested not unkindly that Alex should keep enough to get himself a case of beer from the bootlegger, because he might need it tonight. When Alex said nothing—he was considering drawing to an inside straight, what the hell—Roman leaned in closer than he had the whole time and asked loudly, in an exaggerated and deranged way, "Why?"

Did he mean why draw to an inside straight, or why any of this at all, but Lyle Green took it to be the second one and announced, smiling, "I'll tell you why. The boy's dyin' for your sins is what he's doin'."

It took a moment to register, and then, though he didn't like Lyle Green at all, Mr. Tate laughed. Roman Burkitts never did get it, even when Mr. Tate turned to him, pointed to Alex and said, "It's Eddie Christ."

About this time Eve came in, followed closely by her father. Their timing suggested they'd heard about the state of affairs and had come for the finish. They stood side by side, shoulders touching, father and daughter. A quick look up at Mr. Gartner and Alex saw something absent from the man's eyes. Most of all he looked tired, but he also looked at ease. Alex tried to imagine what they'd talked about.

Eve came over and put her arm around his aching shoulders, not knowing she was adding painful weight to them. Her eyes were tired and sad, but she was smiling when she said, loud enough for the others to hear, "I don't know about you."

She opened a bag and took something out and held it under his nose. He used his lips like fingers to take the piece of smoked mackerel. He chewed while working on turning two pair into a full house. The full house didn't come, he put more money in and now Eve was feeding him a dried apricot. He ate two, then shook his head, enough. She put her hand to his forehead, which felt prickly and hot and was probably red, because she dipped her fingers into his water jar and gently wet his brow.

Alex stared into the screen and played. He had come to the conclusion that his mum, but not his dad, might have liked this game. He emptied his bag and spread his remaining coins on the counter. Eve touched each one quickly and told him, "Twelve."

He looked down at the coins, which no longer seemed real. In this light their brass colour could have been gold, they could have been ancient coins bearing the stamp of Caesar, or something just as fantastical. They were almost gone—but he knew they had never really been, they had come to him simply as tokens of his finding fish for grateful people, and he was as content with this idea as he had ever been with anything.

He stopped playing and let his fingers rest gracefully on the buttons. He smiled looking at the coins. They had taken on a glow. He knew now what luck was, how it came of truly not caring if you had it or not. And, knowing this, he saw that if he kept playing he would start to win, and keep winning, and ruin it all.

SEX IS RED

MORRIS WAS IN A DEMON PHASE, refusing to walk home alone from grade two, and Marie Anne was in a chaos of hurry, circumnamulating the kitchen island while trying to debone a chicken and talk to Cath on the phone without getting bird-grease on it. A hair dryer propped on the counter roared into a snowboot to dry it for her walk up to the school. All day she'd been contemplating the possibility that Morris might be a growing misanthrope, that she was raising an apprentice asshole, a drag to live with for another decade. His demon phases were getting longer, smarter, and more cruel.

The knock came as Marie Anne worked her foot into the wet boot, picturing the hunched, impatient boy of yesterday's walk when she'd said to him, If you won't tell me what's bugging you, how can I help fix it? He had looked at her like it was she who needed fixing.

It was one of those knocks that come just as the door is already being opened from within.

Here stood Tooley, twenty years later.

"Mary."

Marie Anne hadn't been called this since the west coast.

"It's Mary. Look at you."

"Tooley?"

Tooley nodded rapidly, smiling, eyebrows way up. "This is a wild little moment."

He was shivering. His nose was red, eyes wet. One eye had a flash of yellow under it from a recent black eye. He had on a little windbreaker.

She tugged its flimsy sleeve. "So you must be from Vancouver or something."

He nodded quickly again and laughed.

"This must be New Brunswick. I got the good socks though."

He hoisted a pant leg to show his green and orange polka-dot sock. Tooley being proud of his socks. It was as if he had taken two decades to cross the country to show her the latest socks.

"You're freezing, come in!" Then Morris's sharp face appeared to her. "I mean, no! I have to go! But you come in. I'll be back in twenty minutes. Have to go get my son!"

She was ripe with nerves, shaky. Here was Tooley, and everything was too much in focus, the pair of them standing at the door, communicating with nothing but convulsive little laughs, and she had to go get a son named Morris. Tooley smiling, teeth bucking out a bit, which had always been the friendliest, the most vulnerable thing. Dripping nose, cheap red running shoes of a man half his age, curly hair all over the place as always, but grey in it now. Stupid little blue windbreaker. She had run away from Tooley and hadn't thought of that escape in years and years. She realized now how it would have hurt to.

"Jesus no, I came to see you. I'll come with you. You have a son?" He reached for her hand to lead her out.

She pulled him in and ran for one of Lawrence's sweaters. Tooley took the heavy, bone-white cardigan, held it to his small shoulders and laughed. Lawrence outweighed him by probably eighty pounds. Marie Anne explained her lateness and hurried him into it. She felt an old irritation rise as she watched him take his windbreaker off, put the sweater on, discover the windbreaker wouldn't go over it, take off the sweater to try the coat under instead, hurrying now and missing sleeves with his hands. One wild arm came within an inch of the Bissonette plate cradled in its brass stand on the antique hutch. Marie Anne watched this, her hand on the doorknob, smile automatic. Tooley. Time was the thinnest film, and it had just ruptured and was gone.

The rented house was cheap and small but had four bedrooms. For years Marie Anne had one and Tooley another, while the other two rooms saw a turnover coinciding with classes starting or ending. Tooley, the only nonstudent, had a job in a building supply yard, and was considered the responsible adult of the house, which didn't describe him at all.

Marie Anne was studying anthropology, and her passion lay in fragments of bone buried in the ground. The day she moved in, and the psychology student roommate asked her, "Why here? Don't they have dead Indians in New Brunswick?" Tooley stepped in to ask back, "Don't they have head problems where you come from? Why didn't you just stay and study your parents?" It was more a goof than a challenge, and the logic didn't really work, but it made the roommate smile and change the subject, and Marie Anne was to learn that this was pretty much the effect Tooley had on people.

He got confused and smiley about the simple, practical things, like paying bills, or even putting the bowls where the bowls should go, and at first she assumed he smoked a lot of dope, though that wasn't the case. She saw his shy fuzziness had hidden, bold plains. Like the loud socks under the cuffs. Or the anger that rose flexed and unapologetic at any injustice. Or the first time Mary—it just seemed natural to change her name here—explored the back yard and looked up to see Tooley framed in his bedroom window, smiling out at her, his curly head shaking a little with the smile, an intensity aimed at nothing in particular. The constant hint of teeth was not unsexy. The rest of the house was light brown, but this back wall, his wall, he had painted sky blue. It clashed with the grass and everything else, but couldn't be seen from the street.

"Quite the house." Tooley looked back over his shoulder as they walked, and his statement was a question asking exactly what it was she had done in the past twenty years to wind up in a situation like this. "I thought the Maritimes was poor."

"My husband's vice-president of the university. Lawrence."

"Ahhh." Tooley glanced back again, adding, "Wow."

"Anyway, so what, so what are you doing way out this way?"

Tooley looked down and hesitated, which scared her a little. He didn't laugh after saying, "That's an interesting question," and this scared her again.

"Nothing, then, in particular? Just cruising around?"

"More or less."

Cruising around New Brunswick, midwinter, no car, in a windbreaker and sneakers. It had begun to snow, filling the dark gaps in the knit of Lawrence's sweater, and catching in Tooley's wild hair as if on hooks. The school was just up the hill and around the corner.

"You, y'know, still into digging up bones?"

"Jeez. No." Marie Anne smiled, but the question had blown the dust off something forgotten and left it so clear it was shocking. It was like seeing with an old pair of eyes. "Not in a long time. I just sort of dropped it. And then became a mom." "Now you grow them. Little bones." Vintage Tooley. "Morris? Was that his name?" "Morris. There's his school." And there was Morris. Standing alone and exposed and angry out at the corner.

He began to give her little looks at evening meals with the two other roommates, daring comic winces out one side of his face whenever Randall the psychologist bragged or chewed with his mouth open. The first time Randall pronounced statistics as "stastistics", Tooley found her bare foot under the table and pressed it with his stockinged one, the wool softer for the moment than it was gaudy.

So it was obvious, his attraction to her. She wasn't sure how it would rear its ugly head—that was how she thought of it, as the cliché—picturing a kind of clumsy, faceless knob of yearning rising up at her in public, sort of like a penis manifest in human form. But neither was she clear how she would answer it. Tooley was a different sort. Boyish and showy on the one hand, on the other he had roads that might twist on inside for miles. Marie Anne—Mary—had had lovers enough to know that seeing a mind's limits was even worse than getting bored with a body.

The first spring, the front yard grew a dangerous hole—an ancient septic tank collapsing. Their landlord had the work done, but the excavation company didn't finish up, leaving a square of nude earth. Rather than tell the landlord, Tooley seeded it himself, a ten-by-ten square of chives. The sprouting did look like grass, thick, slightly cartoony grass, but soon it spiked up high and uniform and rubbery. If the breeze was right you could smell onion. Then the topflowers came, and their yard had a foot-high green cake with mauve frosting. Standing on the porch, studying the colours, Tooley said, "Nature doesn't usually give you a good clash like that."

And one evening after a bottle of wine, just the two of them home, Tooley asked her, "Ever had a roll in the chives, little lady?" They went hand in hand to the chives, he John Wayne, she the giggly gal, and they rolled. It was only a long joke, and he was so unlike John

Wayne, how could she not? But his sudden rigid squeeze wasn't unexpected. She pulled away. Not because she didn't want to, but because she could feel how he wanted to so badly. Back in the kitchen, Tooley smiled and said, "Oh well."

When the landlord next came by Randall had moved out so they blamed the chives on him. Tooley told the cursing man it was all part of a "psychological experiment", and this didn't surprise the landlord at all.

"Y'know, the guys are gonna call you Moe," Tooley said, breaking into the hard silence of mother and son. Morris wasn't speaking to her. She had tried to apologize and clarify, but then had grown mad too. It was snowing harder and the wind was beginning to gust. Because of the snow in it she could see the wind's curls and dips and long rushes over the school's playing field. She thought of the phrase, Hand of God.

"Ever hear of the Three Stooges? Moe was the leader. The smart one. A bit of a meany though."

Morris was looking up at him, interested. Tooley seemed unaware of the effect he was having. He looked dully into the snow, hands over his ears. Maybe he was subtle and great with kids, the kind of wise-advice type you saw enacted on TV.

"Why?" asked the boy.

"Why was he a meany?"

"No, waddy do was mean?"

It was one of those moments. Marie Anne heard the car come up just as Tooley was putting one hand over her son's face and drawing its middle finger back with the other. Lawrence honked just as Tooley grumbled in a Bronx accent, "Why I oughta," and let the finger go, snapping Morris on the forehead.

The electric window on the passenger side came down. Lawrence leaned across the front seat at them, shouting, Hi Buddy! Morris ignored his father. Scowling but eager, he looked up at Tooley and yelled, Ow!

Should she get in back with Tooley, the guest, or up front, in her customary seat, with her husband? Lawrence had just come upon a strange scene, she didn't want to add to his questions. She got in front, and Morris sat in the middle, climbing over her, boots and all, which he knew she hated.

It felt impossibly hot in the car. Lawrence had just put out a cigarette. She could feel Tooley alone in the back, and even for these few seconds there was too much silence.

"Got off early, and this is a treat for me," Lawrence said, moving his bulky shoulders as if truly excited. "I never get to drive my Buddy home from school." Then he looked crisply into the rearview. "Hello."

Marie Anne introduced Tooley as an old friend from school. Tooley was polite enough as he reached up and shook the big man's hand, but his face was utterly blank, and Marie Anne knew her husband had already been judged. She was careful not to catch Tooley's eye.

"He hit me in the face," Morris announced.

"He didn't, Morris, he was joking," said Marie Anne, who couldn't not watch Lawrence.

Morris looked at his father too. "He hit me in the face. He's stupid."

Lawrence shifted in his seat. His leather coat croaked.

"Hey. Moe." Tooley had Morris quickly from behind by the shoulder and the boy turned around to him, scared. "You really have to lighten up a little bit." He gave the shoulder a firm little shake. "Or I won't call you Moe any more."

Marie Anne watched her son turn back, scared and infatuated.

Tooley suffered through a half year of heavy drinking, which led to two serious fights downtown—strange to contemplate in a man as thin as him. He declared this a wonderful lesson and quit drinking altogether, with ease and good cheer. He also quit his job. Taking only part-time work, he spent his time gardening, hiking in the mountains, and "just enjoying", as he put it, "the beautiful place I live." He would come home with a motorcycle, and later trade it for a ten-speed; his hair would be a lush and wild mane and then he'd show up head-shaved. "I am unencumbered," he would tell anyone, more goofy than bragging, but suggesting nonetheless that while they were in school taking on knowledge and credentials and other burdens, he had already achieved what might conceivably be life's goal.

Head down in her work, Mary had a peripheral sense of seasons, of casual boyfriends, of Tooley's haircuts. Trips back east to Bathurst, term projects, roommates coming and going, leaving their mismatched dishes and shedding chairs. During her fourth year, Tooley told her she was no longer an Acadian, because she no longer said "ting" for "thing".

They were best buddies. Tooley was always home, always a friend in his fuzzy, shaky way. Because of Tooley, Mary liked coming home. They talked about everything, her problems, her doubts, and after five minutes with Tooley she could laugh at failure itself. They'd never mentioned the roll in the chives, for it was clear to both that if she ever changed her mind, here he was. Though Tooley had occasional lovers, Mary was careful never to bring men home. It was strange to live in such proximity, knowing that, among other things, his accidental glimpses of her underwear-dashes to the bathroom might be troubling.

"I am completely unencumbered," Tooley repeated to Mary one evening at the edge of a noisy party. "Except for one thing." He turned it into a joke, adding, "Except for one ting." His eyes on hers, his eyes trying to go into hers, he left no doubt about what the one encumbrance was.

She could have handled it differently but Lawrence wasn't an easy man. He was kind, but he wasn't easy. If things went too fast for him he'd hold up his big hands, say, "Wait a minute. Explain something to me." He'd be smiling, but he'd mean it.

They were in the garage. The electric door descended behind them, squeezing off the snow-laden wind. Tooley had said "Wow" at the door's opening as they approached it, and Lawrence of course had noticed this. Marie Anne found herself wondering if perhaps Tooley had been a long time somewhere, maybe living north, in the bush. Those hikes of his into the North Shore mountains.

"Where's your luggage?" she asked him, as Lawrence taught Morris a high-five routine after Morris successfully turned the key, shutting off the engine.

"Jesus, so who gets to cut all this firewood!"

"Where's your stuff? Where are you staying?"

Lawrence stopped to watch Tooley in the rearview while Morris kept hitting his father on the hands, then up the arms, and once hard on the cheek. Lawrence grabbed both his son's wrists, and the boy struggled while his father watched in the mirror.

"No, I didn't come to stay with you."

"Well why not? Tooley, where are you staying?"

"No. No way." Red in the face, Tooley smiled and searched furtively for exits.

"C'mon, we'll just go get your stuff."

"Seems he doesn't care to, Marie Anne," Lawrence declared, grinning and heaving his shoulders as if in a laugh. "Leave the poor man alone."

"Well, you have to stay for dinner then. Please? I don't think I ever cooked for you. It's my fantastic chicken crêpes."

"Puke," said Morris.

Tooley looked at her. He hiked up Lawrence's sweater, reached into his windbreaker pocket and brought out a balled pair of socks. Bulky, home-knit, a faded mousy brown, but an intricate, raised pattern in the weave. X's and O's.

"This is it. My stuff." Smiling, more a goof than a challenge, he held the socks up to her face. "But they're an heirloom," he added, the socks now the object of everyone's intense focus, all of them sitting hot in their coats , in the car, in the strange leather light, the car contained in the firewood-stacked garage, outside of which they could hear only the flailing hints of a snowstorm.

She cooked for him occasionally, and one time in particular, the Friday evening of her graduation. It was a perversity she enjoyed, that of doing things for others when it was she who should be fêted. Out of this same perverse spirit, on her graduation night, after cooking a tourtière, she said she had a present for him, and gave him her Haida bone amulet on a chain.

"I have one for you too," Tooley said. He took her hand and led her from the table. When she saw he was leading her to his bedroom she was truly surprised, and laughed. She drew him back to the table to retrieve her wineglass and bottle, and then let him guide her where he wanted.

His deadpan quite professional, Tooley paused with his hand on the doorknob and said, "I saved up for this for a very long time."

Afterwards in the kitchen Tooley's mood was exuberant, even though ten minutes ago while they lay naked together she had spoken of leaving. But as he stood there now in his underwear, forking up the rest of the tourtière right out of the baking dish, as if they'd been lovers for years, his mood was wide open and non-stop, which was just like his love-making had been.

"That was like, that was like a carnival in there," Tooley said, eating, staring off, shaking his head in wonder. "There was so much going on."

"There was." Marie Anne nodded and finished her wine.

"I mean, our past. Our friendship kind of mutating on the spot. A wild, wild, new body. Our smells. My stupid, pathetic gratitude! Everything staring us right in the face." Tooley looked at her, smiling now but still shaking his head. "It was great but it was almost too much."

"It was." She remembered his wide-open eyes, and she remembered closing hers. During sex she liked darkness.

"It's gonna be harder," he added, casual as could be, still smiling and still her friend, "because the animal part doesn't forget."

All evening she could hardly keep up with him, that mood of his. After the last dish was dried and put away he declared that the one thing this house had been lacking all along was a good middle-class set of matching dishes. In fact it was probably for this reason and this reason alone that the people living here were all so damned transient.

Tooley had two spray cans of fire-engine red rust paint. They laid newspaper on the front porch and spread the dishes out, a few dozen in total of plates, bowls, cups. They stood bent over as they sprayed, each with a can, a first coat, then a second.

Then stood on the porch in the evening cool, holding hands, examining their work. Rich and blood red, the dishes actually looked pretty good, as art. Food might not look all that great on them. And of course the paint would eventually come off. Holding a plate to his corny breast, lifting his gaze, Tooley proclaimed that these dishes were a portrait of his heart, and that as the paint got chipped and worn away, so would his heart fare as the time and distance between them grew greater.

Then he dropped his gaze and simply stared at her, his eyes wide open in confidence—eyes that did have roads twisting on inside for miles, eyes that all along had been inviting her in, and now dared her.

Mary looked at him just long enough to know that she couldn't. She looked down to the dishes, nudged a plate with a foot, and a bead of paint ruptured and bled onto her toe. The redness of the red was frightening, and clarified things for her.

"Then one day," and now Tooley's eyes damned her, "they'll

just be dishes again."

He dropped the socks in her lap and Mary spun around in her seat in surprise. What she saw in his face made her panic and reach out her arms for him, even in front of Lawrence.

Tooley fumbled with the door handle but got out. He stooped back in to say, "Bye Moe," then walked to the closed garage door. Pondering its wires and pulleys and how it might be opened, he removed Lawrence's sweater and laid it on a stack of cut birch. When he saw the side door he didn't hurry getting to it. Nor did he look back at the car. He opened it and walked into the snow, which blew almost horizontally now. By the time he closed the door behind him, Mary was crying.

She was crying and squeezing the socks that smelled of hand soap, and she was angry that time was what it was because already the fabric of her life was edging in as she remembered the deboned chicken waiting on the counter. And she wondered what she should tell Lawrence, and Morris for that matter. Her husband was sitting there rigid with eyes closed. Morris looked like a baby again in his fear of his mother crying. Should she tell them she was crying because it was possible to forget a lifetime? Should she tell them she was crying because that man's face had horrified her? That his face was a dead blank, and her life had been judged, and they were part of it? Or should she tell them that that was a man who had waited twenty years to get revenge?

THE NIGHT HE PUT HIS CLOTHES ON IN PUBLIC

THE PARTY WAS NOT SANDY'S IDEA. They suggested his place probably only because there were no longer kids there to disturb. It was the annual birthday thing, for him and two others with birthdays around the same date.

Maybe he could be excused for what happened: people act up when to dos are made. Once he'd broken a knuckle, for instance, years ago at his bachelor party, and the scandal was that in the morning nobody, not even Sandy, knew how it had happened. Friends had been embarrassed for him. But big deal. Other people did far worse—one hears about affairs with house fires or strange injury or weird diseases in the family. Odd accidents happen constantly to some people, everyone knows a few and hears the fresh rumours when their lives move down some new dark alley.

In the week that followed the birthday party, he saw that word had gotten around. The tumbling fall, the torn fingernail that bled on the clothes. On the street he saw people he didn't know looking at him sideways. Churchy old women made a big nose-up not looking at him at all.

Why had he done it? It wasn't the divorce. It wasn't even losing the kids to her. His lawyer—years back they'd taken the same commerce class together—he could've killed, true, the man's incompetence was plain, but none of that had anything to do with what happened at the party. He'd been drinking, but so what. Maybe he was just bored. Maybe he'd been bored for years, maybe the pressure had built up and at the party a valve blew. God knows what boredom— Take boredom and add hormones and you get vandalism. Take boredom and poverty plus some religion and it's war. Take marriage and boredom, creeping goddamn boredom, a woman criticizing you for so long even her sneer's nothing more than boring—

But it couldn't have been boredom. Sandy recalled being excited. Up, feverish, angry. Maybe it was his excitement that made him hurry down to them, maybe that was why he fell. Tumble-tumble. How it hadn't hurt, man.

He'd been trying to say something to them. Though now he saw that putting on the clothes was a strange choice of words, so to speak. Had they understood his little lecture? Because that was what he'd been doing, he was clear on that much: he'd been trying to send a message, a symbolic message. Falling sort of ruined it, turned the messenger into a clown.

It was awful, an awful party. Potluck yuppie casserole dishes crowded his kitchen counter, talk of fresh coriander and such pretentious shit, pasta this and pasta that, you didn't hear the word noodles any more. Stink of garlic as lids were lifted. Him a stranger in his own house. Under the spotlight. People trying so hard to be completely normal to him. He heard whispers of "Donna" several times, and a "why didn't Donna go for the house?" and once, he couldn't believe it, he heard either "his wife-beating" or "his wife believing". Which was it? He wouldn't put it past them.

He hated what these people had become. These days, as soon as they ran out of things to talk about—couldn't argue weather or politics any more, both had gotten so weird—they began to talk about each other. They had become judges. Some of them had somehow found what they thought were tools for judging. Words like "denial" and "empower" flavoured their speech like the new spices they pretended to know about. Beech—big, bearded Robert Beech—was the worst. "I'm only trying to help." Right.

Sandy stood up against the curtains. He wanted to step behind them. Listening to Beech, he saw why he'd stopped going to these parties. It wasn't just the Donna thing, the not getting along in public. No, some time over the past years, what used to be called "spilling your guts" had become the thing to do. When someone like Beech dropped his voice and described the royal mess he was inside, when he did the bit about his father's suicide especially, he did it proud he had the balls to admit such stuff and the rest of them didn't, though they were just as messy, or worse. If Beech got his way, parties turned into goddamn contests where tired adults who deserved a decent Saturday night dug inside themselves to see who could spill the most degraded bit of gut. Who can get most naked? Who can goddamn dangle their goddamn parts in the spotlight?

Which was what happened tonight. Sandy was getting a little drunk but mostly angrier and angrier, standing pinned to the curtains by Beech. As if knowing, Beech had stolen his favourite chair and was holding court in it. Sandy had been refusing his questions for years, and here was Beech trying even harder to get him under the lights. As if Donna and her bruise—one fucking bruise—was their business.

It came to a head when Beech asked him why, after being a part of this group for so long—they'd known each other since high school—why he still wouldn't talk about what mattered. That is, about himself. Why hadn't he ever discussed his problems? His marriage going bad. How did he feel about his kids, no visiting rights at all? What the hell happened? Sandy! What's happened to your life? I mean, why won't you ever go past chit-chat? You can talk to us. It helps.

Sandy squeezed his bottle. Beech had gotten so slick at this. Sitting there like a priest, his forehead all shiny. He loved being asked this stuff himself, so he could flaunt and spill. Tonight Beech was greedy and savage and had him pinned. What, Beech asked—Beech's nose so close that if they'd been rats Sandy could have gone for it, bit into it and ripped it, it would have been allowed, it would have been *expected*—what, Beech shouted, are you afraid of?

Then Sandy was upstairs, inside his closet, flailing away. Breathing hard, brain roaring. He couldn't recall climbing the stairs. Below, he thought he could hear people leaving, though he didn't know if he'd said anything, done anything, to Beech or not. He was just suddenly standing up here in the walk-in, panting, amazed at all the colours he owned.

Somehow he had acquired a thousand hues and tones. And, strange—they all seemed to go together perfectly. Maybe that's why he did it: all his clothes simply looked good together. Didn't that make sense? When held up side by side, two very different colours might seem to clash, but when seen with all the shades in between, the rainbow of hues that eventually blends green to purple for instance, the link is obvious, and seamless. And maybe, like colours, a man's moods, a man's contradictory behaviour—even violence—could be explained in the same way, that there is a logic, a rightness no one else sees, and if only the bastards could see all the little things, the mind-beating bullshit you put up with endlessly, behind closed doors, there are always reasons for what we do, good reasons, there is a seamlessness to it all, and before anyone lays blame, well....

He knew he had to put on the tightest first. He knew what he was doing. He was smiling. It was hard work, fabric dragging against fabric already on. Smiling, big bubbling grin, on the edge of a guffaw.

He saw her stuff where she'd piled it on the floor—she hadn't even come back for it, said in court she was too scared to, nice ploy—and he decided to wear it too, had to rip all his stuff off because hers would be the tightest. All the static electricity in doing that—crackling, popping, lights going off in his face, actually hurting his cheeks. But he began again, he put on the six pairs of panties and the lone pair of pantihose, the fishnet things with the black seam she would wear as a kind of slut-joke. Then her two cashmere sweaters, one black and one sky blue, old dead gifts from him, their sleeves pulling halfway up his forearms. The sweaters made him instantly hot. Soon he was sweating freely. Then he was into his stuff again, T-shirts, at least eight of them, and maybe fifteen white dress shirts. Then the suit pants and then the cords she used to have folded on the bed, ready for him when he got home from the bank, then the baggy, splotched painter-pants, and finally two pairs of sweatpants. His knees couldn't bend. He couldn't stop smiling. Then his grey suit jackets, he ripped a sleeve on one, so what, he had lots. This was still his good old house, these were his good old suits. Then six more sweaters, each one harder than the last to pull on, each one forcing a louder grunt. Last, a cardigan that barely stayed on, a burst rind. Then his ties, his thirty-one ties, in order on the rack, one for each day of the month; he'd done it for years and no one, not even her, had ever bothered to notice. It was hard, but he knotted them all properly, his deadened elbows, elbows big as flowerpots, clanging the empty hangers on either side of him. One side being "her side of the closet," a cute idea at first. What a big stiff ball he was. But it wasn't a joke he was grinning at. It was a growing feeling. He knew he was feeling a freedom. That armour gave. He sensed the brotherhood of knights. We lack armour today. On went the old windbreaker with racing stripes, which she hated and years ago hid in the back of the closet, in a box. He found a sportscoat he'd missed and, pulling it on, ripped the back open. His mother's old mink was here too, Donna had left it, correct to the end; it was a big square thing, luckily his mother was fat. Then all his winter clothing. Then three Hallowe'en masks, covered by the big rubber Margaret Thatcher head, and all that topped by three hats, the last a huge floppy quilted thing with earflaps, from his time on the Prairies.

No coat button was even close to its hole. He tied up the whole mess, his huge colourful self, with a lamp cord. The lamp dangled and banged around his crotch. There he was, almost perfectly round.

It took several minutes to manoeuvre the bedroom, mostly to get through the door. "Happy Birthday" was being sung downstairs, probably some stupid lit cake was being walked in. He discovered he had to pee badly, was faced with the choice of undoing everything or—

He decided in one second. He peed smiling. It was wonderful. A huge and thick piss weighted by so much beer. Some of his layers were waterproof. No one would ever know, it was freedom. He was diapered, a baby again, a treat unexpected, sublime. He closed his eyes, so safe.

He felt the spreading warmth. It felt like being forgiven. It felt like being forgiven everything.

And then he was at the bottom of the stairs. They thought he was unconscious. But his eyes were closed because he was still marvelling in his fall. He was trying to keep it going, the softness, the bouncing down the bones of the loving body of his house, which had not hurt at all.

His eyes were closed for this and other reasons. It was horrible how quickly they undressed him.

THE AND

IN THE POLICE STATION WALTER BONNER WAS MANIC, and in the car he kept up the nervous quips. Driving, Don couldn't help but notice how big Walt had gotten, how he sat with legs apart to accommodate the stomach in true fat-person style. The balding and the frizzy little ponytail only made you see his fatness, like a high heel used to make you see a leg.

"Can't believe it." Walt's moan was more excited than despairing. "They impound my car. I mean, I'm stupid. A gun."

After finding the marijuana they'd opened the trunk and found an old .22, along with dirty blankets and rusty camp stove and other unused, ten-year-old junk. What Walt said next was a joke, mischief in his eyes. "I mean, who knows what else they'll find. It's a party car. You ever been in that car with me on a weekend, Donald?"

Not knowing what to say, Don asked if Walt wanted to come back to his place. Walt shrugged assent as if they did this all the time, as if it hadn't been years. Then he kept raving—were they really forty, his weight, homegrown, how strong it had gotten, remember way back, that time Don got so high he started hitching "just west", penniless and barefoot?

Walt flexed a shoulder and winced. "*Jesus* that guy grabbed me hard." Face pained in a deeper way, he added, "I think he *wanted* it to hurt."

Don suspected the cops had meant to humiliate Walt more than anything. Shame an old doper, smarten him up. That they had demanded bail was odd. The five hundred wasn't much, a formality, but Don had been under the impression that anyone caught with a bag of dope these days was fined and sent home, a "misdemeanour".

Lousy demeanour—a sneer or bad posture.

"Nice car," Walt said, rapping the dashboard with a knuckle. Don nodded. He did like his Lexus.

"Still surveyin' for the City?" Walt stared out the window, eyes flitting but unconnected, as if it mattered to them alone that they register each car, house, tree.

"I don't get outside much any more. Been office bound for years."

"The boss man."

"I give the orders and everyone hates me pretty much, yup."

"Weird job you got—I remember you saying this yourself— 'cutting the planet up into imaginary squares and people taking them seriously'. I always thought that was a good one."

Pulling into his driveway, Don only vaguely remembered a time when he'd seen his job that way. It was strange that Walt Bonner would remember and not him. Looking down his street at the row of driveways—imagined rectangles people took seriously enough to pave—he recalled how he used to be good at that sort of stoned insight, a mix of funny and cynical and a bit of dire, and how he could get his friends smiling. He remembered being called Wirehead.

He ran water for coffee. Watching his old friend pace the living-room, the obese man jittery like he'd survived a car crash, Don decided to go with Diana's decaf. He watched Walt slow up at the CD shelf, head tilted to read titles, sounds of recognition and surprise.

"They have a new album? Donald! Why didn't I know this?"

"Diana's brother sends stuff from England."

"But a whole new *album?* Gotta be a bootleg."

Like he was still nineteen. Even calling him "Donald," like the old days. The longer version of his name had somehow been funny.

Watching Walt at the CDs, Don understood. For better and worse everyone else had grown older, but Walt not so much. He worked at a record store in the mall across the river. It was all he'd ever done. He'd started up his own used place once but otherwise he'd always worked in Fredericton's record stores. He looked nothing like the other salespeople, all of whom were young, but Walt's music-knowledge was something of a known commodity in town.

"You still like Bruce *Cockburn?*" Walt had been driving to work when arrested and was wearing jeans, white shirt and black vest, the hip uniform. "Donald, come on. I mean, the guy *babbles*." He smiled waggling the CD case at Don. "This is his little *soap*box."

Odd in the first place, Walter Bonner calling him out of the blue to please come bail him out. It spoke volumes and what it said made Don sad. He and Walt hadn't socialized in twenty years. They bumped into each other on the street, had coffee maybe once in the last decade. What did it say about Walt's life that he had no one else to call?

Walt said, "I mean, *listen*," and put on the Cockburn. Don listened, and now that he considered it, Cockburn did squeeze lots of syllables in, a man with a message.

Walter Bonner had a perceptive wit but it had always been aimed at the peripheral. A man without plans unless they involved the weekend. He no doubt blamed his lack of women on his body, but the true culprit was his mind, it was *him*. Don had watched girls, and then women, recoil not just from the beer-burp humour but from the constant trivial joshing about details. What beer to avoid and why. How a band's new label was ruining their music. Absorbed in the details of leisure, Walt argued its details even when there was no one else arguing.

Walt, who had taken a seat as though to enjoy the music, started shouting over it.

"Donald! A *bumper sticker!* You believe it? A *bumper* sticker!" He lurched to sit up straight. "An '*and*'? I mean, come on, man, *you believe that?*"

"Well, that's not what you got arrested for."

"Yes it is."

"They didn't bust you for a bumper sticker, man." Don felt the word "man" in his mouth, how long it had been.

"Yes they fucking did. That's exactly my point. I'm screwed. I, am, screwed." Still smiling.

"It's maybe just a fine. There was hardly any."

"Kevin's wife works with lawyers. It's going to get back to Kevin."

"Kevin?"

"My boss. Straight as a chopstick. I'm late all the time anyway. I mean, *dope?*" He shook his head.

Don heard the front door open. Nita and Max. He caught Walt's eye, put a finger to his lips. It took Walt time to comprehend. Kids, to Walt, probably meant only that the parents couldn't party with him like they used to.

Juanita came in doing a little dance that mocked the uncool Dad-music. She had this way of popping her hips that made Don queasy and, surprisingly, reminded him that she was adopted. Nita stopped dancing when she saw Walt. Max came in too, and Don realized it was Max he especially didn't want hearing that his father's friend had been busted for dope. Max was fifteen and expert at pushing walls, and he could easily twist the information into something like permission. Nita, on the other hand, would see Walt's age and ugliness and not want anything to do with any of it. She would see the affair as tawdry, and she would be right. A fat forty-year-old who worked in a kids' world of music, careless baggie on his car seat, busted like a teenager and now ranting about injustice.

"Hey, good moves," Walt yelled at Nita, and Nita smiled. She and Max both looked interested in Walt. The clothes, maybe. Or maybe he was a kind kids liked. Santa. Laughing Buddha.

"Nita? Max? Walt, an old friend. Walt? Juanita and Max." As he always did at times like this, he saw Nita's darker skin through Walt's eyes.

"Hey," Walt shouted, "what kind of music you like?"

Pathetic, it was all the man had.

"I mean—" Walt grinned wickedly and yanked his thumb back—"you like this?"

"Yeah, right," said Max. Nita smiled and rolled her eyes.

"So who ya like?"

"I don't know," Max mumbled. "Pumpkins. Soundgarden."

"Ministry?" Walt leaned forward, his look mischievous.

"Sure." Max nodded at the floor, impressed by something, but Don didn't have any idea what.

Walt turned to Juanita and said, "And you..." He hesitated like a judge. "...love Alanis!"

Watching his daughter blush, Don felt the flash of jealousy. Music was touching his kids as it once had him, and he didn't know what they liked. Max, who did little but irritate him these days, who faced everything with that stupid knowing disdain, might have a pure passion going with some band or other and Don was missing it completely.

When Don mentioned that Diana would be home in twenty minutes and would he stay for dinner, Walt seemed for a moment nervous. He passed on dinner and, seeing Don was into peeling vegetables, wouldn't let Don drive him home. He patted his belly and said a walk would do him good. He was visibly excited again, his manner at the door suggesting that he didn't know what would happen next in his life, and that maybe this walk home was going to be part of the adventure. Don recognized this brand of excitement. It was of an era.

Walt left, but not before he gave Don a soulful look, said, "Thanks, man," and shook Don's hand in the old hippie way, that thumb-up, brotherhood clasp that Don had never in his life instigated, or felt anything but self-conscious doing.

After dinner he told Diana all about it, how Walt had this bumper sticker, a police public relations one that said, "Try Hugs Not Drugs," how Walt had replaced the "Not" with an "AND" in red paint, and how this prank had attracted cops like flies to a turd.

"Here's this beaten-up car, this grungy ponytail guy driving it, this *invitation* to pull it over—of *course* they're going to search it." He almost added, "Just to hassle him," and it would've been another word he hadn't used in years.

"So's this friend Walt a daredevil or just stupid?" She'd heard Walter Bonner's name before, when Don and his friends were into beery stories.

Don shrugged. Stupid, sure. But a better word to describe Walt might be "innocent". Or "hopeful". Though it didn't make as much sense, "hopeful" felt like the one.

Don remembered when, a few years back, Walt's name had come up a lot, a brief flurry of Walt. On the radio, both Don and Wendel had heard a voice they agreed had to be Walt's phone into the campy Saint John oldies show and request Percy Sledge's "When a Man Loves a Woman". The DJ asked if there was a dedication, and the Walt-voice said, "Absolutely. Love to Carolyn." According to gossip, Walt Bonner had been pursuing a co-worker, Carolyn, in spectacular fashion. Roses, gifts, now Sledge's love-howling. Don envisioned a probable case of Walt looking at her and seeing destiny, her looking at him and wincing, the affair never making it to a coffee together. The next gossip to come out of the mall had to do with a harassment complaint. Walt ended up fired, then got his present job in the mall across the river.

"It's a brainless message anyway," Diana was saying. They

were into a bottle of wine. "I've always hated it."

"What?" Don had only half listened.

"It's a stupid jingle that makes no sense."

"'Try hugs not drugs'?"

"Well, who's it for?"

"I guess it's—"

"For kids it doesn't make sense. They're supposed to drop their chunk of hash and go hug somebody? Who—parents?"

"I guess."

"That's realistic. When's the last time Max came up and hugged me or you?"

"It's just a general, feel-good message," Don offered, stung by a notion that the days when he'd been allowed to touch his son at will were long gone. But he smiled at his wife, who for some reason had taken up Walt's banner and was on a wise-cracking roll with it.

"Joey Streetkid's supposed to go hug his girlfriend? That's why the lads smoke dope till they see pickles in the sky in the first place, because all their girlfriend *will* do is hug. Or they can't *get* a girlfriend."

"I guess the 'and' is more appealing."

"Hugs take two. Teenagers don't have two. Being alone is what makes them teenagers. It's a stupid bureaucratic pun and it creates heroin addicts at first sight."

Don nodded, smiling.

"I'm serious," Diana said. "Fluff like that does more harm than good. It *makes* them do drugs."

"Reefer madness."

"Well precisely."

Don silently disagreed, believing it was simple old fun that made you do drugs, but he thought of his own favourite example of a time he first saw authority not just as fallible but stupidly so. It was third grade and the principal had called an assembly to lecture them about snowballs. Half the school was by now aware that the principal's car had been ambushed that morning. (Don had been one of the throwers. And, come to think of it, so had Walter Bonner.) The thrust of the principal's message was that if you threw a snowball at a car, the car would go out of control and kill you. Rigid with menace and sibilance, the principal hissed into the mike, "*One thousand pounds of sliding steel.*" Don found the guy's tactics disgusting. Was there a kid so idiotic he'd stand in the path of a car to throw a snowball at it? As for it hitting you after getting pelted, it would have to do a tight U-turn, double back and then plough through the five-foot snowbank you were hiding behind. A driver couldn't get you if he tried.

"But to have that bumper sticker, and dope in the car," Diana was saying, shaking her head.

"He forgot it was there. I guess he smokes a lot."

"Like you and me that time at the border."

Don finished the wine in his glass. The bottle was done but he felt no pleasure from it. And he knew the wordless struggle was coming. A Friday night, Diana would want to open another bottle and he would say he didn't feel like it himself but leave unspoken his wish that she stop now too. She would get tipsy, then sloppy, and he would make an excuse to get in his car and drive, maybe go through a car wash and fill up with gas, maybe end up like last week at the 7-11 aimlessly thumbing through magazines.

Don suddenly felt old. Severe and humourless. How many years ago had he lost the notion of "Friday night"? Diana still had it. And somehow Walter Bonner had been allowed to stay back there all the time, in that old world that had mostly to do with chasing pleasure. Don remembered it to be a simple world, one in which you were restless but not particularly unhappy. Authority was the bad guy and freedom still had meaning—it was an urge you felt in your body and it formed the way you stood or sat or moved. You were often in a car going somewhere, the radio on, the radio music was good then and you were nodding your head to the beat, the music a perfect sponge for your restlessness.

Even Walter Bonner's weight seemed to point to wildness, to some kind of freedom.

"Walt has reduced the whole sixties thing to one word," Don heard himself say.

"What."

"'And.'"

He said it as a joke, but at the same time he knew he meant something deeper, something he understood more with his body than his brain.

"Another one?" On her way to the recycling bin Diana flashed him the empty bottle.

"Okay. Sure," Don said, surprising himself. Diana was visibly pleased with his answer, and he wondered how much he would have to worry about her in the years to come.

"Red," he added. "We have some red, don't we?"

"Yeah, though we're not really eating anything...." Taking a bottle of red from the cupboard, Diana didn't finish her objection. She screwed the previous cork off the corkscrew and began opening the new bottle, a Hungarian subtitled "Bull's Blood". She put it between her legs and pulled, gritting her teeth. Don had wanted to say something about white wine being for middle-aged bureaucrats and red being for horny Italian poets and he wanted to be a horny Italian poet tonight, but he'd thought too long about how to say it and now it wouldn't come out funny.

Fredericton was small enough that it was no surprise that Don's next news of Walter Bonner came from gossip overheard in his office: the fat record-store guy across the river was up on drug trafficking charges, had been fired from his job and had moved back home with his invalid mother.

"That's where he belongs," one secretary said to another.

"Well, exactly," said the other, though from their voices Don heard that while one meant the mother needed help, the other suggested Walt Bonner's childishness.

That evening he phoned Walt at his mother's. It occurred to him while punching the buttons that he had dialled this very number over two decades ago, probably setting up weekend plans. Standing with the phone to his ear it all felt too sharp, a snapshot of time itself, time too condensed. He could feel the age of his hand. He could feel the weight of the flesh on his face.

It had been a month since Walt's arrest. He'd been meaning to call, and not just because Walt hadn't gotten the five hundred back to him. In fact he was willing to blow off the loan in the name of old friendship. Five hundred might be a problematic amount for Walt. Or Walt might have simply forgotten. Don could easily picture Walt's world still being like that.

Walt's hello sounded thin and scratchy.

"It's Don. Just seeing how you were doing."

"Donald. Hey. Doin' not too bad."

"Sounds like you have a cold."

"Yeah, maybe I guess I do." He laughed at the coming joke, and coughed. "I'm sleeping on this couch, right? And I can actually feel this draft coming up between the cushions. There's like this cold line across my back."

"Your mum's, eh? That must be a little weird."

"Tell me about it."

"Your mum doing okay?"

"Yeah, in the sense that you get used to having no legs."

Don had no answer for Walt's sad chuckle. He had a notion of inviting Walt on a trip, one of those brilliant escapes where you just jump into a car and drive, either south to warmth or to Montreal or Boston, the strange bars and music and the tang of people a little more dangerous than you. Holding the new phone against his old face, Don could easily see Walt in the seat beside him, sipping a can of beer, the two of them shaking their heads over the absurd angles in their life stories. He pictured himself asking Walter Bonner: does the fade of sex mean that marriage was only about procreation after all? And, tell me, Walt: if you have less feeling for your one begotten son than you do for a girl you adopted out of Peru, what does it say about race, what does it say about gender, what does it tell you about goddamned blood and fatherhood altogether?

Had this been any of his other friends, Don might have suggested such a trip, and they both could have moaned about how great it would have been. But this was Walt so he didn't, because Walt would have actually agreed, would have been ready in the time it took to find whatever money he had and gather a bag of cassettes.

"So. Do you—" Don felt his clumsy tongue. "—if you need some money or something, lemme know. I heard you got fired."

"Yeah, eh? My boss—"

"Kevin."

"You know Kevin?"

"Well, you— No."

"It got back to him. He's straight as a chopstick. Bang, I'm gone."

"And it's trafficking now?"

"*Completely* bizarre. They found this leather pouch full of seeds. A gift from this guy way back. I mean, some day I was going to plant them, maybe, or cast them into the wind or something, Johnny Appleseed, I don't know."

"Right."

"I'm no farmer, right?"

"No."

"So they jump to major conclusions. Here's these little seeds and to them it's like a year later and they see bales drying in a barn somewhere and a bunch of kids lined up to buy." Walt laughed. "And the gun really helped."

"What's your lawyer say?"

"Ahh, I dunno. Who knows."

"Well I hope it goes okay. I'd be surprised if much happens."

Walt didn't answer, and Don felt stupid. Much had happened already. Walt had likely exhausted the record stores in town. He was over forty with no experience in anything else at all.

"Anyway," Don said, meaning to end the phone call, "if you need a place to crash or something." Crash, another one of those words he had never used without seeing himself using it.

"No, this is perfect," Walt said, deadpan clear in his voice. "Kerouac went back to live with Mommy right about this age. I'll write a novel."

"Right."

"But I mean, it kills me. Kerouac was Canadian. He was basically a Canadian. But it's like he's this huge American icon, right?"

"I guess."

"Neil Young, Joni Mitchell, Céline, Alanis—small potatoes, man. We should be hanging onto Jack with all our might."

It was impossible Walt was talking like this, impossible he could be interested in anything but his own bad life. Don didn't know if it was just a weird joke or if Jack Kerouac had in fact gone back to live with his mother. But what exactly did it mean to be out in the world for years and then go back to your mother? There were no words for that sort of failure, though it occurred to Don that everyone knew exactly what it felt like.

The next day Don phoned a friend, Larry, a prosecuting attorney. Later Larry called back with news about the Bonner case.

"They were watching him and they got him."

"Who was watching him?"

"Well, the cops."

"What do you mean, 'watching him'?"

"I don't know. I guess 'aware' of him. You said he was this old party person."

"Well so the fuck *what*."

Larry paused at this, and Don, embarrassed, heard his outburst echo in his ear.

"Maybe his name comes up," offered Larry, "I don't know."

Larry added that though the .22 was a separate issue, it did colour things. The details of the trafficking charge were too arcane for Don to make much sense of, but it involved an almost poetic interpretation of the nature of seeds, how in a seed lay the intent to grow it. And since the marijuana represented by the seeds was too much for one person's use an intent to distribute was equally assumed. A big fine and some prison time might ensue if the case was used to warn off others. Local cultivation had become a problem.

"Yeah—a problem for Jamaicans and Colombians," Don said, surprising himself.

"Sure, I guess," Larry said, then he had to go.

Don came away from the call angry, a conspiracy against poor Walt. He had a sudden headache, but one that felt familiar, as though it had bloomed from the root of a hidden headache he'd had for years. How was Walt in any way dangerous? "Watching him." Watching what? A guy floundering along looking for fun.

Headache pounding now, Don phoned Walt again. He let it ring seven or eight times and hung up to a vision of Walt's mother trying to nap. Where was Walt? Don had no idea what Walt did in a day, where he went, who he saw. He felt the urge to find out, and recognized the feeling as the one you used to have when you suspected there was this great party somewhere and you were missing it. Which was absurd—of course it was—to think of Walt's life as some sort of party you were missing. It all had to do with middle age, the glare of these doubting-years. Typical, missing an old life that memory had cleaned up to look way more fun than it had been.

But what was it about age that first of all complicated fun and then made it impossible? He discovered he was standing, staring out his office window. The view might as well have been a wall. Walt, what was your fucking secret, man?

He wanted to leave the office, leave early, something he never did. A boss putting in the longest hours was one good thing a boss could do. And if he left where would he go? Go home and swallow some aspirins. He pictured home and felt the weight of it. Diana with her flood of details that didn't matter to him; Nita reading a book, a girl-book that had nothing to do with his life and she knowing this even more than he did. And Max. Max, headphones on, upside-down in a chair, his look suggesting Don's mere presence was judgement.

He sat, tapping a pencil on his desk, staring straight ahead, nowhere to go. This was where he was. He saw how he was stricken with the fact that he was stricken. He sat up straight when he understood that it wasn't Walt Bonner who was depressed.

He woke more severely hung over than he had in years, perhaps ever. He stumbled to the bathroom to gulp water and then throw up painfully. He made his way back to bed aware it was Friday, a workday. Hours later he was awake again and lying in pain with only vague, dark recall of last night. When Diana came in to deliver some orange juice her smile was a bit fearful.

"What happened?" Don whispered.

They'd gone to Rob and Clare's for dinner, he remembered that much. He remembered more as Diana talked. The Bordeaux they were drinking had reminded Don of a month he'd spent in that region years back and he'd waxed nostalgic and more or less guzzled. They'd ploughed through five bottles, surprising everyone.

"You were great," Diana said, and Don saw she was hung over too. "You got everybody in the mood. Though we have to get to Rob's and pick up my car sometime today."

She continued her recounting. Rob and Clare had a bunch of liqueurs to sample and Don didn't want to stop.

"You kept yelling for "Let It Bleed", and Rob kept having to tell you he didn't have it."

Don moaned, though it wasn't so big a thing.

"You also kept asking for dope. You made Clare check every nook and cranny for dope. You forced us to all get down on our hands and knees. You were pretty funny. 'I know this house is full of roaches!'"

Don suffered recall of being on his knees. He remembered handling a crusty old pen and sticky pennies.

"You kept yelling 'Hugs and drugs!' 'Hugs and drugs!'"

"Jesus...."

"No, you were funny. You suggested group sex—"

"Ah, shit...."

"You were funny. You wanted to call up Walter Bonner and get him over there and everyone have sex with him to make him feel better. You were kind of surreal. You did kind of scare Clare."

"Jesus."

"What *wasn't* fun...." Diana put her fingertips to her forehead and stared into her palm.

"What."

"What wasn't fun was you yelling at me."

"Why was I yelling at you?"

"That's what I was hoping to ask you."

"What was I yelling?"

"You started out kind of funny. You yelled at everyone, 'I'm done!' Over and over. Like, I'm drunk, I'm out of it. 'I'm done.' But then, then you sort of singled me out. You grabbed my shoulders...."

Diana turned away. It looked like she might cry.

"What? What did I do?"

"You kept yelling. 'I'm done!' Right into my face. It became sort of a snarl...."

"Was it—that bad?"

"Well, it was the reason the taxi got called." She looked down at him, her anger sparking again. Though it still seemed to him she was talking about someone else.

"God...."

"Don—do you want to talk about, about something? Is something on your mind?"

He moaned, and tried to think.

"No. I really don't think there is."

Diana looked satisfied enough by this. She stood up.

"Boy, you sure were drunk."

"Appears I was."

He ate and showered and as the afternoon faded he began to feel less hellish. Diana wanted to take advantage of the kids being over at friends' but he couldn't for the life of him imagine having sex feeling like this. He didn't mind the headache, which was logical and deserved. It took him till well after dinner to feel less guilty. He helped this along by absorbing himself in chores he'd been ignoring lately—dirty windows, the squeaky closet door.

The next morning, Saturday, he rose early from a good sleep. His headache was gone. He decided to go in to work and clean up yesterday's business. On the drive over, the radio was full of live news about some guy on the old train bridge. There were unconfirmed reports of a gun and someone wounded. The area was blocked to traffic and people were being warned away—which of course made Don want to drive there.

At his desk he went through files for ten minutes before he realized he was profoundly uninterested. Unable, in fact. He tried to read, to focus, but he couldn't. It was as if his eyes and the words were opposing magnets, forced apart. The effort felt quietly awful, and threatened a tunnel into which he might fall, face forward. He drew back and for a moment thought he might throw up. He quickly jammed all the paperwork into the top drawer. He was sweating freely, had been for some time but only noticed it now. He shut his eyes to take deep breaths, then put his forehead onto the cool surface of his desk, rolling it back and forth, slowly at first and then speeding up, and then so quickly he knew it was craziness and had to stop. When he picked his head up he studied his office, which was tidy and quiet. So cleanly geometric. Even the electric light was formed by its square fixture. The only lines that weren't perfect belonged to the potted plant, a jagged palm-like thing. But its inclusion in the decor seemed strategic, making everything else look even straighter than it would have otherwise.

The sudden thought that the gunman on the bridge was Walter Bonner made him stand up so quickly that the chairback banged the wall. He was smiling.

In his car he leaned towards the radio, aiming an ear at it. The DJ announced "Six in a row" and on came a neo-disco thing that was so irrelevant it sounded evil. He switched to the Saint John station, all oldies today, and "Brown Sugar" was on. By the song's end he was downtown and he could see the river between the buildings. At a barricaded intersection people had gathered, many craning their necks as if to see around the buildings to the bridge. He parked in an alley and got out. He had no evidence it was Walt, but it was Walt.

The cop at the barricade was too rigid with duty to answer questions other than to announce sternly that there was "one individual with a firearm".

A bug-eyed man of about fifty turned to Don to say how surprised he was that "the SWAT boys" hadn't gunned him down yet. "Spray 'im," he said, putting his long face up close. Don could smell fresh toothpaste on the man's breath. "Lunatic's standing out the middle of the bridge. Open up and spray 'im."

"You've seen him?"

"Course I seen him."

"Was he fat—?"

"Got up in there behind a tree, SWAT boys called me away. He's just standing out there on that bridge. They should *get* the asshole."

"Is he *fat.*"

But the man was already walking and he gave Don a snort and an odd look, as if his question was crazy or meant to test if he'd seen the gunman at all.

"*Hey,*" Don yelled, loud enough so several bystanders looked at him, "*fuck yourself.*"

He walked two blocks and craned his neck a few times himself but couldn't see the bridge. He felt sweaty and nauseated again, but smiling eased that. He got his car and then a coffee at the drive-thru. Pulling out, blowing into his paper cup and gulping the coffee hot, he switched from a BeeGees song back to the local station, on which a voice emphatically outlined the facts so far. A young woman hospitalized with a foot wound. The shooting perhaps accidental. Gunman possibly suicidal. But still considered dangerous. No names as yet released.

In the middle of the block two pedestrians suddenly ran out in front of his car. Other people were running down sidewalks, pushing past the barricade. The radio voice, its new baritone betraying urgency, interrupted itself with, "He's in the water. He's jumped. This just confirmed. The gunman has jumped."

People running by him, Donald let the car roll along at idle. He let it roll and roll, watching the street disappear more and more slowly under his hood. How far would it roll? He bounced with silent laughter. He was aware of honking. When his car did stop he sat still, taking seriously the unmoving road, a rectangle with no end to it.

YOUR FIRST TIME

1969 AND I WAS SEVENTEEN. I'd been in bars but not this one—The Niagara down on Hastings. Pretty bad. It was early in the season and the first time we'd gone out together after a game. Most of us had the new team jacket on—shiny red and stinking like fresh plastic. I worried that us being here at all would invite some sort of trouble, and I was right. All these sick junkie types and hard-core greaseballs. We looked like a collective dare.

Our waiter, rough himself, came up and asked, "Kiddies?"

Dale, who was twenty, and who three years down the road would play a few games for Boston, told him to just keep them coming. We all threw two bucks in the middle. Draft was twenty-five cents.

So we began to drink and get to know each other better. At first it was hard to forget where we were. I don't know whose idea The Niagara was. Maybe it was known for not checking ID. One shock to me was the long hair there. I loved long hair—and mind expansion and the whole thing—because I was drifting in that direction. I had the longest hair on the team. And I was the youngest—a kind of new generation. My hair wasn't long-long, though some guys took runs at me during games. But my notion of long hair was violated in The Niagara. I'd never seen it on guys who looked fresh from jail, and ready to go back. I hadn't learned yet that beaded and shampooed hippies were more or less suburban.

After a game it doesn't take long. Pouring beer into a body crying for fluid—you might as well be injecting it. We were soon so loud I couldn't hear the loudness around us, the music chugging from cheap speakers, the clicks and curses from the pool tables, the low roar of fifty grease-bikers doing—I imagined—deals. We were louder than all that. We had won, we were tough together, we were rising in beer, peering into the bliss. Lords.

We relived some of the game's memorable bits. Coady, a small winger on the checking line, didn't score much but he'd scored tonight— while screening their goalie he was crosschecked in the back of the neck and on his way down a long shot (mine) went in off his ear. Every once in a while one of us would look at him and go, Hey, nice goal! and Coady'd roll his eyes, his ear puffed and scabbing, no way he could move his head, and we'd haw haw. Then, to me, Hey nice pass! and we'd haw haw some more. We looked pretty wild—red-faced and quick-drunk and laughing, our hair styled only by violent towelling.

It wasn't long before Dil Carnback started singing. Dilly was our pet Swede, a cousin of L.A.'s Juha Widing, who'd convinced him that junior hockey in Canada was the best route to go. Dilly was a good enough guy but he was always way off the mark. Definitely alien. Singing now in an eager, big-eyed fashion, glancing around, urging us to sing too. He'd picked up on something he knew, a Beatles' oldie, "I Wanna Hold Your Hand", coming out the bad speakers, and he was a foreigner ready to party. We looked at him blankly, and he mistook our scorn for density because he got even more eager.

We let him sing. How do you explain cool to anybody? It's like art, all feel. Dilly missed the point on the ice too. He was our best scorer, and might in fact have made it in pro if—well, little did any of us know that tonight he'd played his last game. The point is, he was strong but had no sense of appropriate force. Blind to the flow of a game, he'd absolutely cream a guy, a non-threatening nobody, face in the glass, for no reason, in the neutral zone, and he'd wonder not only why he got a penalty but also why he got no accolades back on the bench, where he'd look around for the praise a good smear could get you. Or during that brawl, everybody dropping their gloves and a few guys going at it but mostly just orderly shoving—Dilly speared the guy he'd partnered off with. Guy drops his gloves and Dilly spears him. Didn't hurt him, but still. Dil couldn't respect a fair fight because he was too freaked out to see one.

We drank and laughed and drank, the table never not loaded with beer, and there was Coady laughing too, neck anesthetized now.

A bum approached our table, and it was funny because I actually sort of knew him. He had the long coat and all that, but he was

only about forty and sort of handsome. I knew him from the movie
line-ups he worked downtown; my girlfriend's big sister was a social
worker and knew his name: Jim Pal. When the night was young and
he wasn't yet flailing insults from the garbage of an alley, he'd approach you with this great Bogart schtick—"I need shum coin for
shchool, shee? Shay, howse about contributin' to an education?"—
and I could hear it now as he worked his way up our table, palming
quarters, glancing up fast every two seconds—a mouse in the cat
food—to make sure a waiter hadn't seen him.

When he was a couple of chairs away I called, "Hey Jim!" sort
of as a show-off to the guys. He startled, and looked at me a bit fear-
fully, but then he plopped down beside me in Dilly's vacated seat. I
thought, oh great, and some of the guys were laughing about my "new
friend".

Looking hard at his feet, Jim Pal said, "Talk to me."

"What?"

"*Talk to me.*" A frightened whisper.

I considered options. He began talking exaggeratedly loud. "So,
Pete, what you been up to since, ah, my brother's place?" I saw the
waiter's legs come up and stop behind him and I realized Jim Pal was
using me to, in effect, hide.

"So you up to anything new, Pete?"

"Well, Jim," I rolled in, talking too loud too, "I've dang well
gone and got myself engaged to be married."

The waiter's legs moved away. Jim Pal slumped in his seat and
sighed. He didn't thank me, but he said, "Bastards here beat the crap
outta me one time." He picked a beer off the table and looked at me,
raising his eyebrows in question. I said sure, and heard Dale yell, "Aw
man, get *rid* of him."

Jim Pal hoisted the beer in a toast. "Blindness," he said. He
flicked me an ironic glance and—though you got a glimpse of awful
teeth—this playful smile.

He definitely had a charisma to him. You could see how he
could support himself panhandling. He buttered you up but you liked
it. There was something meaty going on behind his eyes. He looked
bored not only with me, but also with our table, the bar, his situation,
the night. He understood it all and it didn't excite him. I had recently
read something somewhere suggesting that anyone you met might be
the Buddha, that they might be the ugliest, weirdest creature imaginable, that they wouldn't admit they were the Buddha, and that in fact

they might not know it themselves. I neither believed nor didn't be-
lieve this idea, but it did make you look twice at someone like Jim Pal.
"You guys all gonna play in the NHL?" he was asking me,
sipping his beer. I wasn't sure but I thought I'd seen his hand move
fast, so this might be his second.
"Some of us, maybe."
"That your ambition?" He turned and looked at me, amused.
He was really quite handsome, but with three days' beard, and a smudge
of tar or something on his forehead. His eyes were sane.
"I guess so." I paused. How to brag modestly? "They say I have
a decent chance."
"Who's they?"
"Scouts."
"You're too soft."
"What?"
He didn't answer. He knew I'd heard. I wanted to tell him that
it was true I wasn't a great fighter but I could throw a check. I was an
offensive defenceman in any case, like Bobby Orr. Well, a slower, off-
key Bobby Orr. But I could lug the puck and make the nice pass. I
could—
"You're not mean," he said, smiling. "It's not a bad thing. It's a
good thing." His eyes brightened with a joke, which he delivered as
Bogart. "Kid, you're too damn good for the NHL."
Con or not, I found myself interested in this bum's opinions,
but Dilly was back. In fact he'd been standing behind Jim Pal for some
time.
"Sir," said Dilly, all worked up but still foreign and polite, "this
is my seat that you are sitting in. *So.*"
With a "Hey, no sweat pal," Jim was up and gone and out the
door. He didn't acknowledge me as he left. It looked as if a few bills
were missing off the table. I realized the "Pal" name might have been
stuck on him because of his routine. I was quiet for a minute. Sitting
next to him, you could sort of feel his awareness coming off him, as
though it was a burden he tried to shed every night. He knew things I
didn't.
I saw I was gulping beer down. In drunk and corny tribute, I
thought to myself—blindness.
Suddenly there was a game going on. We were to take turns
telling our "first time" story. Tell your first fuck, was the instruction.
We were getting to know each other.

Dale went first. He volunteered so fast that you knew he had a funny one. Actually only the telling was funny—he couldn't stop laughing and it was contagious. He took a while getting to it, but the gist was that in high school this gorgeous girl he'd had a crush on for a year finally agreed to go out with him, grad night no less. He was so nervous he drank and drank and passed out in the woods, where the group had gone for an all-night fire. He came to with her all over him. The woods, the dirt, her prom dress. When his story was over I could tell it had all been a way for Dale to brag, that he still loved her and was proud of her though she was long gone.

Danny Smallings went next. We were moving along the table in my direction, and I was four away. Nervous, I started thinking about my story. My first time? There were those early, fumbly ones, the stuff some girls led you to so they wouldn't get pregnant. But I guessed that your first time meant penetration.

Smallings was laughing out his story the way Dale had, but Smallings was mean and not liked and the story didn't have the good feel to it. I caught the phrase "So she comes with me to this *furnace* room, right?"

I didn't want to tell about my first penetration-time, because it still made me feel queasy. The whole next day I'd felt sick. A soul-sickness. I hardly knew Patty, it was a party somewhere, I knew she'd "been with" guys, I'd heard she had a crush on me, I asked her upstairs, we were up there maybe only five overwhelming minutes, I never did have my pants right off, and then I was downstairs and making excuses to leave, and I left feeling lousy, and felt awful all the next day. The next time Patty's name came up it was because I was being told she thought I'd "treated her like a whore". She was probably right. I remembered in the bedroom saying both "I'm sorry" and "thank you", trying to cover all the bases. But I knew she didn't really like me either. How could she? We'd had no communication at all, no chance.

My second and third times went pretty much the same and I began to suspect a major Victorian guilt, a kind of refusal to accept the animal I became. I'd see myself and hold back. Much like my fights in hockey—the other guy was always better at being an animal.

I missed what Smallings ended with but the guys were laughing, and Smallings added, "I mean, what a *pig*. What a *hose* hag."

Stan Michaels, a tall, shy defenceman, sat pale and blinking, aware he couldn't get out of going next. He had a girlfriend of long standing, Cindy, who came to the games and waited quietly outside the dressing-room for him. She was as tall as he was. My guess was that there'd been no one other than Cindy—in fact I had my doubts they had even done the deed. Stan's nickname was, simply, Two, his uniform number. I thought the name a pretty witty comment on his colourlessness.

Stan swallowed, took a deep breath. Hard to hear, he began with, "There was this girl up at the lake where we go with Mom and Dad every summer."

Interruptions of, "It was Cindy, right? It's Cindy."

I looked around us at other tables. I'd been reluctant to look before, afraid to meet anyone's eye in this place, but I was drunk enough now and how could I not feel safe? Some of us, Smallings especially, and Dale, were on the team mostly for their toughness. And the game was all about sticking together when it got rough. So I looked around. The place had thinned out. We were by far the thickest, loudest table. A bouncer had a pool player by the arm and he was saying, as to a child, Gimme the stick. Right behind us one very skinny biker chick was passed out, face-down on the wet red terrycloth table. No—her forehead hovered an inch above the terrycloth. Shit, her eyes were sort of open.

"...so we canoed," Stan was saying, "we canoed to this, this island...it was sort of a picnic, you know, we had sandwiches—buns and, and cheese...actually her sister was supposed to come too but—"

"I didn't know Cindy had a sister!"

"What's Cindy's sister's name, Stanley?"

Stan smiling now. "This isn't Cindy."

"Yer sure as fuck in trouble then!"

"We're tellin' Cindy!"

I didn't catch the ending to his story, which received a mock cheer and a "Way to go *Cindy!*" because I was rehearsing what to say. I still didn't know what story to tell, because if my first time was depressing, my second time was bizarre, as it had also been my first time with psychedelics. I shook my head thinking about it. Me and Heather in the park, middle of the night, the wet grass. Things starting off romantic, ending in a panic.

Everyone perked up and stared at an eruption of shouts at a distant table, a few of us standing up as if eager to join in, but no fight materialized so Kenny Doak, our goalie, began his story. He was twenty and married and you could tell that sex was no big deal any more. His first time he'd been twelve, he said, and everyone had a good time with this, gibes about all goalies being strange. By definition. What a job description, etc. Kenny's nickname was Target.

I was deciding to go with my second time. The more I thought about it, the more I got giddy. LSD—I didn't know these guys well. I knew two of them had tried grass once. The others, what would they think?

The funny thrust of my second time was that I'd been worried about "performance"—coming too soon—and being stoned and hyper-conscious had made it way worse. I'd read about a tactic whereby, if you felt in danger of coming, you visualized the least sexy thing possible. I tried this with Heather in the park, and of course on acid my visualizations were effortless and colourful and swept me away. I tried "rolling in broken glass" first, and I was instantly cut and bloody and worried about dirt and bacteria getting in my shredded body. Just barely realizing that I had control of my fantasy and not the other way around, I switched to eating pancakes with my parents on Sunday morning. On I went, trying my paranoid best to "perform".

Kenny Doak's story was a story only for its punch line, which was that he came before he even got it in, "wrecking her goddamn dress", and she yelled at him and literally kicked him out of the car. Kenny finished with a beaming, "So, hey, does that count as my first time?"

I got up to go to the bathroom, striding between tables that aimed faces of scorn and malice. No one within twenty feet of him, a guy in a biker jacket was laughing out loud, but insincerely, like he was only advertising himself. Some tables I passed I knew not to look at—from the corner of my eye I could see the challenging stares. One guy, not much older than me, dressed like the kind of hippie I still admired, smiled gently as I went by and asked, "Downs?"

The bathroom air felt broken and dangerous. One guy was just standing there in the middle of the wet floor. I didn't dare look at him. I peed with difficulty, alert. As I finished I heard a gasp from a cubicle, and from the adjacent cubicle, or maybe it was the same one, somebody chuckled and said with affection, "Fuck you."

You could hear our table from across the barroom. No one in charge had changed the tape, and "I Wanna Hold Your Hand" had looped around again for the fourth or fifth time. The place was in flux, random silent people slinking in to sit or stand, looking for something, then slinking back out into the night. It was the kind of scene

I'd get used to over the next few years, but without a team.

Back at our table, Dilly Carnback was about to begin. Then me. I was almost eager now, because I knew I'd make a few of the guys a bit nervous, a bit thrilled. I was ready. It was weird in here. My story would fit the night.

And I'd doctor it a little. Exaggerate. The delay tactics—instead of rolling in broken glass, I'd make stuff up. They'd get a kick out of this: screwing away, afraid of coming, I imagine myself playing hockey, all the colours so bright in the arena, the fans cheering too loud, I have the puck behind the net and a guy chases in one side so I go out the other, carrying the puck, everything is so vivid it's like I'm really there playing hockey, that's what acid's like, I'll explain, and I fake a pass and get around a guy and suddenly I'm in the clear, I wind up for the big shot and—boom—the goal grows hair and suddenly it's a giant vagina and the puck slides in way too nicely, and now of course I'm back in reality again, inside Heather on the ground, and *oh no* I'm going to come, I have to think of something else quick—OK, a face-off, game tied, a minute left…. I envision the guys laughing, shaking their heads at me, the adventurer.

Dilly's story was boring and the humour incomprehensible. I listened impatiently. I thought, Hey, I'll beat him no problem, and then I laughed at myself out loud. Which made Dilly laugh with me too, and nod eagerly in encouragement.

His twisted, European details made the table uncomfortable. He was losing his careful English and getting hard to understand, but there was some kind of family wedding, maybe even a sort of royal wedding, and he went on and on about "a grand smorgasbord, *grand*, with these wee, these wee, how do you say in English, rolled beefs, *baby* beefs…*veal!*" The girl's dress was "a very light yellow" and her hair "too casual for the occasion."

"Come on, fuck her Dilly," someone urged.

A few guys had turned to talk among themselves. Then we all turned to a noise, the face-in-the-terrycloth biker lady yelling to herself. A little biker guy beside her was smiling, shaking her arm. I was afraid of losing my audience, or the game petering out altogether. I couldn't decide whether to end my story with what had actually happened—frightening and depressing at the time, but in the telling it might be funny. What had happened was, I'd done such a good job delaying, going off into visions for who knows how long, that when I came back to reality the final time there was Heather under me, her head flopped to the side, mouth slack, whimpering, "When ya gonna stop, when ya gonna stop...." I'd halted in a panic, apologizing like crazy, and—for all my worry about performance—never did come. Maybe I could end my story like Kenny Doak: So does that count?

Dilly ate too much smorgasbord and the girl was mad at him for some reason and wanted to go home. Her breasts were "like a young-young girl's", and this detail in particular made us dislike Dil Carnback now, and all Europeans, because it was perverse. The women who fit these stories were older than us, they wanted it more than we did, and they had big ones.

Shouts to buck up again. There were no more bills on the table and full beers were sparse amongst the empties.

But then Dilly and the girl were in some room somewhere and doing it on a bunch of coats, and then they were doing it a second time—Dil Carnback was OK again—and Dilly went back for some more grand smorgasbord and then they did it once more. Dil finished the story by gulping the rest of his beer and banging the glass down, dramatic, done.

"Atta baby, Dilly!"

But some guys were definitely getting bored. I dove in.

"Well I dunno," I said, wincing as if I didn't want to do this, "mine's a bit weird—it was also the first time I dropped acid." I did a shit-eating goofy smile, shrugged, apologized. "I mean, it was a wild party."

A few guys smiled nervously, a few whispered to each other, but one or two were openly admiring—Coady yelled *All right!*—as if I'd said I'd chugged a whole bottle of rye and stolen a sportscar. Hockey players respect abandon.

"Anyway, I'm flying. She grabs me by the hand and takes me outside down to this park—"

"*You fuckin' poison.*"

The biker lady was yelling in a throaty rasp behind us.

"I mean, I wasn't seeing God or anything, when I looked at her I still basically knew it was a girl I was all horny at and not some fluorescent octopus or something"—the guys laughing now, my story's going to be good—"but acid, you wouldn't believe it, it's incredibly—"

"*Fuckin' asshole.*"

Breaking glass right behind me, and we're all on our feet. The biker lady standing with a broken beer glass pointed at us. Dressed in black, long greasy hair, sick-skinny little body. Hovering over her terrycloth, she'd been listening. Her eyes were all sheen and crazy, but deep with hate. She stood gripping the glass, her hand bleeding from it. She wobbled as she stood confronting us. Behind her, her junkie boyfriend struggled to his feet, shouting, scared, sounding Québécois.

And Dil Carnback—stupid Dilly, way off the mark again. Stern, his hand out. He said, simply, *No*. And went to her, misreading what was in her eyes. When he was close enough she slashed, and got one of his.

Our waiter was on her then, a fist cracking the side of her head, and Dilly pivoted at me, half in a faint, disbelief blooming on his face, one eye smashed and part hanging out. Blood down his face already. Then he was on his knees screaming, hands rigid an inch from the damage. Now the blood was on his shirt, a light yellow fabric that made the blood look black. I couldn't move. From the periphery I saw her on the floor getting beaten by the waiter and some of the guys, and the helpless boyfriend was jumped as well, a convergence of red jackets, they punched him down and he was kicked in the head and unconscious.

In the midst of this, a strange sound. It was louder than the rest and almost shut it out. It took me a moment to understand it was me, crying. A rich, foreign sound, and a wild, wild feeling, filling me. It was so new that it would take a few years getting used to, this heart music. Funny how the body knew before the brain that all the pillars were falling.

THE SUNDAY LISE SAW JESUS

LISE HAD JUST GOT BACK FROM Sunday school and was sitting in her holiday whites puzzling over some Campbell's vegetable soup and a tuna sandwich. If her mother saw her eating red soup in a white dress she'd crucify her. But her parents were next door and Lise's troubles were bigger. Though she was only eight she knew that what they'd spent an hour talking about wasn't Jesus, though they'd used the name over and over. It all sounded too easy or something, like rules to a game. When you were good he was like a giant friendly lady, and when you were bad or rad he was mad, worse than Dad. Her little rhyme had failed to amuse the teacher.

At which point Lise began to feel bad for believing differently. That is, for unbelieving. But that man in the pictures. The way they said you could talk to him. Well, you couldn't talk to him. In the pictures the colours were bright like comics. All the roads and lands were dirt, but no one was dirty. Lise had asked if they even had toilets back then. The teacher thought a moment, then ignored her, and this made Lise suspect that the mystery of Jesus did have something to do with toilets, or the lack of them. In any case, the mystery had to be about something not in the book.

The last thing the teacher had said was, "Jesus is still alive." This had made Lise sit up straight and think.

She was still thinking as she ate her sandwich. And as she chewed, back straight, eyes unfocused, her unbelief grew. Jesus had to be something not in a book, something she'd never seen, and which no one had ever told her about. Jesus had to be something brand new.

Lise told herself, as a game, that if she could forget everything she could see right now, plus everything she'd ever seen, plus everything she'd ever heard about, then whatever was left might be Jesus. She tried this, and it only took a second.

It scared her. It was like an invisible hinge opening along the whole length of her body, wings within her. She shook her head in an attempt now not to know, but the shock of knowing only grew. She sucked in a breath and dropped her sandwich into her soup. Her spoon landed on the table and soup spattered her white dress. Lise looked down, the red spots a problem that could wait. She held her breath. Her eyes darted there, then there. She bounced in her chair, expectant. Under the table, Butch whined and thumped his tail.

Lise checked the corners where the walls met the ceiling, where spider nests appeared any day out of nowhere, but she saw nothing new. She studied the sunbeam that made a window shape in front of her on the table, but that wasn't it either. Something in the slowly floating dust caught her, but then she decided, no. It didn't speak. Jesus would speak.

Lise shoved aside her soup, bent across the table, and reached for the zapper. It was just news on some war somewhere, old stone buildings lying in hills of smoking pieces. The TV was speaking and the pictures were new, but it was definitely not Jesus. She had a funny sense Jesus might be behind the TV set, something always felt odd and strong in behind TVs, but she knew that, if she got up and looked, there would be nothing to see.

Then a good idea came. You can feel him inside, someone had said. So Lise felt where her collar pinched. She felt the circulation in her legs cut off by the chair edge. But, no. Listening harder, she detected her heart, which she sensed might give a clue. Its beat was warm and teasing because it didn't change, yet was always new. But that wasn't it either. If Jesus was who they said he was, Jesus would be watching. Not the other way around.

Lise's eyes went to her soup bowl. Something had happened in it. The quarter-sandwich was there, bigger than before. All the red broth had silently entered the bread. Was this something? A lot of church was about bread, especially bread that got bigger on its own.

But she'd missed it. If that was Jesus, she'd missed it. The bread now just looked soggy and stupid. A potato square sat beside it, and on the other side was a broken alphabet G. The tuna, the fish part of the story, hadn't gotten bigger at all.

So maybe she'd missed it. Jesus was too quick for her. Maybe it was always this way.

Feeling hot, Lise looked quickly under the table, catching Butch by surprise. The dog's head jerked up, eyes blinked awake, and a burp escaped his mouth, rippling his lip. Lise smelled it.

What she smelled in it surprised her.

Lise didn't have the words to explain to her parents when they came home to find her under the table, her dress soiled, hugging a dog she'd never much liked and whispering to it, "Jesus". She tried to but she saw they didn't believe her that dog burps were new and old at the same time; the only word she could think of to use was "history". Nor did they believe that sunbeams on the table were Jesus, but only when a cloud moved across and made them start again. And it was too hard to tell them—when she jumped up and cut her elbow on the table and hugged herself and the little blood and said, "Jesus"—that it was about not missing it, not missing the blood when it first came out and talked to you. It was about not missing anything, ever again.

And when Lise told them—she couldn't stop, she had to tell— that she could hear them in their bedroom when they cuddled and bounced together, but that up till now she'd never known she was listening to Jesus, they told her they were taking her out of Sunday school. Lise said that was fine. The only time Jesus would be there, she said, holding her arm and looking at it like a lover, was if it ever got hit by a rocket.

FIRE HEAVEN

"Next time it happens like that," Sharon said, cutting something at the counter, "I want you to look into my eyes."

Though her back was to him, Noel could hear that she spoke through a little smile. That shy way she said daring things.

"Next time what happens?" Noel asked, but he knew.

"You know, when it happens together for us."

"It?"

Sharon turned to him. She tilted her head forward so that the effect was of looking knowingly over the rims of glasses, though she wasn't wearing any. Her impish eyes. "It. The big it."

She was making a late snack for herself. Noel had just emerged from the bedroom, where he had lingered after their love-making, curled naked on the covers, wondering if he shouldn't just crawl under and get a good night's sleep. They had come together again, almost to the second.

"The big it, right." Noel nodded, smiling, wedging past her to grab a slice of her cheese. With the other hand he held his bathrobe closed. He'd lost the sash to it during the move. He stepped back, looked at her, took a bite of cheese—goat cheese, Christ—and lifted one eyebrow to go with the Austrian psychiatrist accent. As a psychologist he was always mistaken for the other, so he mocked psychiatrists constantly.

"Vun vould zink zat zee big EET vould be heenuff by heetzelf."

Doing a gentler, better accent than Noel, Sharon said, "Maybe vun zinks too much to begin vith." She turned back to the counter, playful and not. They both knew she had made the request before, years ago. Noel would not escape it.

Another boy—man? He was sixteen—left Noel's office, hunched into his black jacket. Noel had a small insight: you could perceive delinquency by the way kids wore their leather jackets. For some the jacket was fashion, for others a life. True juves wore leather like skin.

This particular young man, Travis—congenital limp, high IQ, great name for a city kid—was a true, menacing, glowering juve, and prison was in his cards. Though Noel felt bad for thinking this of Travis after just one session. It was the kind of assumption the world made of Travis, and if anyone was supposed to have hope it was Noel. You are capable of the right choices, Travis, Noel was supposed to not only say but feel. He'd just seen too many Travises. Broken home, possible abuse, early booze and drugs, too angry to sit in a classroom. It was as if these kids came out of a burger mould: chewed up, then pressed by the basic shapes of pain. It was almost predestiny.

Ten minutes till the next Travis was due. Noel reread the article about deviance. The writer claimed professionals like Noel were refusing to admit that this rotting society was producing more deviants. Instead the Noels were redefining deviance, so that single-parent families were no longer seen as deviating from the norm and blah, blah, blah. What was the guy's problem? There were barely resources for the "severely" deviant, let alone the "very" and the "moderately". And damn the labels. Kids came to his office as refugees from alleys or Volvo suburbs and their pain was more or less the same.

But, in a way, the guy was right. The victim market had grown. When Sharon landed her tenure-stream position here it had taken Noel barely one week to grab a job of his own.

His next client—Julian, another great name—came and went. These big bad city kids were no tougher than their New Brunswick cousins but their answers were slicker, if grunts can be gauged by slickness.

Noel spun in his chair to scan the bookcase for a book he hadn't thought of in years, over a decade, from school. No way it was here. He had disposed of boxes of books as though they were shackles. During this move he'd dumped boxes more. It was called *Sex and Taboo*, something like that. A chapter on orgasm. He remembered being fascinated. One culture had called orgasm "the little death". The French, probably. Another group, Buddhists or Hindus, saw it as a gateway to enlightenment, not because of the intense pleasure but rather for the challenge it presented, the challenge to stay conscious through it, sort of like a monstrous—that was it, that was exactly how the book phrased it—like a monstrous sneeze.

The next glowering juve—Bill, lousy name, and last name Hrcka—pushed too proudly through the door, took one look at Noel, saw something in Noel's face, and laughed the meanest laugh Noel had ever heard.

They made love four days later, and Noel pretended to have forgotten. Sharon was fresh from the bath, and soon had that soap-and-new-perspiration smell he liked. He found himself simply going for it, not waiting for her at all. He felt the coming feeling—a sweet possibility, then probability, then certainty—crammed his face into the hollow of her neck, went fast then faster then fastest, and came. He caught his breath for a minute, Sharon stroking him and cooing (did her cooing sound half-hearted?) Then he descended to help her find her final pleasure too.

All nice and normal. Once back in their early days when it had happened just like that—him too turned on to wait for her—he had apologized for being selfish, and Sharon had told him she kind of liked it when he did that, when he just lost control. From then on Noel did what he wanted, became either selfish beast or patient partner, either being okay with her. It was a win-win set-up if he'd ever seen one.

Tonight, her head on his chest, not smiling, she whispered in disappointed singsong, "You for-gaw-awt."

Leaving, Travis gave a little wave. It was getting painful to meet him. The equation was simple but profound: the more you liked them, the more you felt their pain.

Travis was starting to like him, too. Though he'd looked hungover today, he had kept that erect way of sitting, a natural dignity. With capricious eyes. A James Dean tilt to the head sometimes. The limp was utterly minor in his life, or more like a neat flaw, a beauty mark. He probably had an easy way with the ladies, but it sounded as if he was true to his girlfriend. (Cyndy, two Y's, what was she like?) Noel saw how Travis might have been had circumstances been different, saw a goofy humour shine through when his guard was down, sensed a passionate loyalty to his street friends.

Travis had opened up ever since their second session ended on a positive note, when he'd looked vaguely interested after Noel announced that he had no lecture for him, no advice even. Noel only wanted to hear what Travis wanted to say. Everyone's different, right Travis? So how can I have a jeezless clue what to say to you until I know who in hell you are? Travis looked thrown by Noel's ruralisms, and had left with a knowing smirk, but he hadn't left angry, or bored. That had been the beginning. You could sometimes identify the start of a relationship.

Twenty minutes till Bill Hrcka. Rather than review Hrcka's file, Noel flipped open the library book *The Jade Cave*. Its subtitle was *The Ancient Asian Art of Eroticism*. The chapter Noel turned to was called "Visit to Fire Heaven", all about orgasm.

There was a traffic jam outside, construction up the street, car horns loud from five storeys down. City life. He was almost used to it. Here in the city, with commuting, they were seeing each other less. Was that why she wanted it? Did it maybe have something to do with this great hive? It made sense that alienation would make her crave intimacy.

He wanted to ask her if that made sense, but he couldn't. He realized he could no longer simply ask.

Why was he so nervous about it? What was he afraid of here exactly? He loved her eyes—clear blue-green. In them, her depth of intellect, or a flash of fun. They looked into each other's eyes all the time. What could be so awful about looking into them while coming? It might be a neat little adventure. Like standing up together on the rollercoaster and looking into the other's eyes as the world roared by.

Noel skimmed an anecdote about Bald Hen Mix, a legendary aphrodisiac. A limp-in-love farmer had ordered a cure, a special mix of herbs, and when the tiny package arrived he spilled it in his barnyard. A rooster pecked some up. For the next two months the rooster did nothing but screw hens, night and day, and such was his lusty ferocity that he pecked their heads non-stop while he screwed, rendering all the hens bald.

Bald hen mix, right. The world did not need bald hen mix. Noel closed the book just as the door opened to hateful eyes. Big Bill Hrcka. Bill Hrcka was the product of an orgasm, a male one anyway. Bill Hrcka in particular should not be given bald hen mix.

They hadn't had sex for a week, and Noel was wary getting home from work. Thursday was Sharon's slack day, so Wednesday evening she tended to treat like a mini-weekend. Sex was often on her casual agenda, and Noel had to admit that he was nervous because of this. He smiled at himself. Like a boy on a date.

The evening began innocently. Sitting on the couch they ate ordered pizza and listened to their new CD player. They'd left a broken turntable and albums behind. Not sharing a taste for the same music, they took turns choosing songs. Making little defences of their choices, Noel insisted this early Bowie was ground-breaking stuff, and Sharon suggested that Prince was great if only for the spectacle of ego.

Eagles, Supertramp, Springsteen's "quiet album", as Sharon called it. Aside from a handful of classical discs, so far their small collection was oldies.

"I have a long one," Sharon said, actually interrupting Noel's pick of a Roxy Music. She put on Ravel's *Bolero,* smiling as she walked back to him, knowing it was a cliché they were about to enter into.

Noel saw that he was drinking more wine than usual. Beside him on the couch, Sharon rubbed his chest through his sweater.

Christ, the terminology in that book. His jade stalk. Her moon cave. The idea was that, in union, it became a jade cave, hence the title. He thought of his cave, his mahogany cave, his office. He had to change it. The floor they occupied had housed a law firm, was done up in neo-authoritarian. No matter that he wore jeans, the dark wood of the place spoke of power, and clients knew the power was not theirs. Ironically leaving Noel powerless to talk to them in any meaningful—

"Dance." Sharon was dragging him up to dance to *Bolero,* which had climbed its way wilder and louder. She snuggled into him, brazen. Noel knew that soon his jade stalk would be in her moon cave. Bald hen mix. This marriage had no need of it yet. He pictured himself humping away and tearing her hair out with his teeth, and he involuntarily laughed against her but didn't explain himself when she asked. He changed their dance to a kind of goofy tango.

Sharon sat on the couch to work at his belt and jeans, which had an old-style button fly. He stood, staring over her head, sipping wine, passive, playing dumb. He did feel passive. And not exactly dumb but—meditative. They were about to do It. Visit Fire Heaven.

It was the peak thing life had to offer. People married for It. At least they used to. His parents likely had, because it sure as hell wasn't a union of minds. The big It. The monster sneeze. You had to trust who you were with, either that or not give a damn what they thought of you, because It turned you into a grunting lunatic right before their eyes. Unless you achieved It at the same time and were blind to each other's—

"So much for *Bolero*," Sharon said. His pants were down. The sudden silence was a little embarrassing.

He remembered in high school being shocked hearing this girl mock her boyfriend to her girlfriends, demonstrating how he jerked and huffed and went into bug-eyed convulsions when he came. Seems she hadn't had It herself, yet. Travis's girlfriend apparently had. From the sound of it, Travis and Cyndy spent a bit of time in Fire Heaven.

"Noel."

And those two juves in the waiting room that time, one of them saying, "...so he splits from her after he rubs off all his fun-skin." Fun-skin, good Jesus. Countless juve fistfights over It. Freud based his whole deal on It, more or less. Some women, especially older women like his own mom, suffered at the hands of clumsy or selfish or embarrassed men the vestiges of Victorian England and never in life did feel It. Some cultures, in coming-of-age rites celebrating the worst male fuckhead paranoia, cut out each hopeful pubescent clitoris that emerged, just in case It should cause a wife to seek out a better jade stalk.

"Earth to Noel."

On her knees, very much of the earth, Sharon was speaking into his limp penis, which she held as a microphone.

"Earth to Noel. Dead rocket. Rocket not responding to command signals."

In the morning he stole two posters—one a sky-blue Colville and the other a garish old Peter Max—from an unused hallway and hung them in his office. They covered some of the wood. Later, when Simpson, his supervisor, came by, Noel asked if he could have his office painted.

"Where?" Stepping in, Simpson made an overtly puzzled face and looked around Noel's office.

"Everywhere."

"You mean," Simpson did overtly incredulous, "paint over

this wood?"

"Sure, why not."

"The wood's beautiful. What's wrong with the wood?"

"I want my clients to be comfortable. They don't talk in here."

"What could be more comfortable than wood?"

"They think they're meeting Winston Churchill in here," Noel said, remembering as he did so that Simpson had no ear for humour, especially the dry and flaky kind.

Simpson looked at him significantly. "Well, whose fault is that?"

Travis missed his appointment, which worried Noel. Ruptures in routine often signalled ugly news. And it had been going so well. Travis might soon take his advice, even if sour medicine like a job, school. They acted almost like friends now. Last time, with Travis complaining about boredom again, boredom being almost the worst thing about the street, Noel had said, "Boredom? Try small-town bird-shit New Brunswick you want boredom," and Travis had looked at him, realizing for the first time that Noel knew about boredom, and loneliness, and the waves of blackness that provoked you, made you do certain things.

They looked at each other like human beings now. Half the time they just laughed about small stuff. Little knowing glances. Trust, a magical thing. Noel saw again that this meeting of minds was his life's business.

But today, twenty minutes later, instead of Travis, Bad Boy Bill Hrcka's severe presence reminded Noel that physical attack was becoming more common. There was a desperation in Hrcka's silence, and all it might take was Hrcka to see Noel as an obstacle to satisfaction. First Noel told Hrcka to take his Docs off the chair, and now he was telling him that switching group homes wasn't likely.

"You ain't gonna help? Fuck, nice, thanks." Hrcka's eyes began to shine and to cross slightly, in angry rapture.

"Well, I could ask, but I already know they won't. They won't see a real reason."

"I told the fucking reason."

"To them it's not a good enough reason. Like I said, to them the only reason is if you got a job in another part of town, and held it for at least two months. To show them. Then you could move."

Hrcka's reason was that he hated two perceived "gay boys" in his group home who were looking at him "funny". Unlikely, Noel thought. The funny looks were probably glances over the shoulder, raw fear.

"Well somethin's gonna happen. Tell 'em that."

The scapegoat for his hate last week had been a caseworker who had ruined his life and the week before it was Jamaican taxi drivers. What Bill Hrcka was actually mad at but didn't know it was being kicked onto the streets of Parry Sound when he was twelve. He talked as if he was proud of it.

"I'll tell them. If you promise me you won't lose it." Give him a formula he might understand. "You have no right to get physical unless they do."

Though it was frowned on, Noel gave Hrcka a ride. Then he joined the rush-hour crawl home.

If you weren't in a hurry, rush hours could be relaxing. They were ideal life, condensed: a goal, movement towards it, a soft chair from which to view your journey. Music or news to colour it. Noel discovered he was in no hurry today. No hurry to see her.

Last night had been one of those quiet, awkward-between-the-lines things. A struggle of awful subtlety. No observer would have seen anything like a fight.

There at the couch, *Bolero* over, Noel had finally concentrated on the matter at hand. Sharon's microphone had grown. But when she slipped out of her skirt and tried to pull him onto the couch with her, he wouldn't. Nor would he let her up. Instead he communicated with his hands on her shoulders his desire for her to satisfy him there, on her knees. It wasn't that the position was particularly demeaning, but nor was it one she would normally have chosen except in humour.

When it was over, Noel's legs trembling from standing through a visit to Fire Heaven, he did try to guide her down, so to satisfy her likewise. But she wouldn't go. She just sat there, said it was okay, she was fine. He sat beside her, still breathing a little hard, holding her hand, feeling disappointment in her thumb's listless caress: he would not make love with her because for some reason he would not or could not look into her eyes as he came. Both knew this, and also that the other knew.

As the evening wore on they did speak about this and that, and watched a movie, Sharon commenting that Steve Martin looked to be a melancholy man. Her manner remained lifeless, void of heart.

Noel sat at her side, not knowing what to say because he didn't know what to think.

And now, driving home, he had words for what he'd wanted to ask her last night. Though he doubted he would ever ask. What, in the first place, the question went, did orgasm have to do with love? If he was to believe his colleagues, a significant number of men could achieve it only if they had a date with a woman's shoe. And then there was sex with prostitutes. There was the teenager alone with the door locked. Hell, there was rape.

Obviously love wasn't a requirement. But there was more to his question. Even when you were with someone else, you basically had your orgasm alone. No, you didn't even really have it, it had you, you were overcome (not a bad pun), you were almost unconscious. But love was about sharing, sharing consciousness. How could you do something so evolved as share consciousness when you weren't conscious enough to flip a goddamn egg?

So the question was not, Did orgasm have anything to do with love, but rather, Could it?

Noel got out of the car and saw over his shoulder the sunset he'd been missing the whole drive east. A glorious, a sky-high wall of yellow cloud dying into gold, the kind of spectacle his mother would say was as great as God's sadness. Noel looked at it and, in a surprising union of ideas, came the words, fire heaven. There it was. Even the contradiction of fire-heaven in the Christian sense, of hell burning in heaven, even that felt right, for didn't such a thing describe the nerve-crucible of sex?

Noel was met inside by a message that she would be late, meetings. He ate alone. When she got home they were pleasant to each other, both of them choosing to be kind. Sharon looked mousy and determined to be a good person above all else. Noel hated himself for seeing her in this way.

In bed they said a pleasant good-night, and she kissed him kindly enough.

Travis missed his next session too, and the following day Noel got the news. Travis was in custody in Windsor, something about a fight. An older guy, an ex-con, had a slashed arm and leg.

Just being in Windsor would have been enough to screw

Travis's parole and sever his relationship with Noel. But it was worse than that. The case, as Noel heard it from Simpson there in the mahogany hallway, was that Travis had driven to Windsor with his girlfriend, and Jesus, she was only fifteen, in the other guy's van. Empty booze bottles found, two roaches. They'd parked in a lot right downtown, and passed out, or whatever, and Travis woke up to his girlfriend screaming at this other guy to get off her, it was pretty much attempted rape, and Travis and the guy start fighting, the older guy is bigger, and Travis breaks a bottle and cuts him once, then chases him down the street with it and cuts him again. It was the chasing part, the second attack with the bottle, that was the problem.

Noel pictured Travis in his underwear, crazy-limping in pursuit of this bastard. Would a judge or jury see—regardless of how sordid it all looked—that what Travis felt for Cyndy was no different from, was maybe even stronger than, what they felt for their own husband or wife? Would they see the purity in his eyes? Would Travis let them see it? No.

Soon Simpson was onto another story about another juve, because the affair with Travis was not so remarkable. But it bothered Noel a lot, he was surprised how much it bothered him. He would have loved to help save Travis. He could bear having a son something like Travis. Travis had some gleam of kindness. Humour that showed his soul. That last session, and now indeed it was their last, Noel had been explaining why, for all its hell, the street was addictive to some kids because of the peer acceptance they found there, and Travis, understanding completely, had interrupted to explain it better, saying, "On the street all the black sheep are white to each other."

Noel drove home thinking of Travis. He decided to go and see him. Travis was now out of his jurisdiction, out of his reach, but he still wanted to see him. Give some visible proof that someone cared.... Who knows what nudge might nudge him the right way? Who knows which irritating grain of sand will make the pearl?

Again Noel was in no hurry in the traffic, even though it was hot and the air stank with things he preferred not to think about. He drummed the steering wheel to an old Led Zeppelin hit. Kids these days still listened to them, apparently. Actually this made two Led Zeppelin songs in a row, maybe one of them had died. "...squeeze my lemon till the juice...." Big guitar crescendo. Primitive licks but a decent raunchy melody. Everywhere, it was everywhere.

Bill Hrcka, whom he probably could save, he didn't care to.

Hrcka didn't drink except for beer, and only if someone bought it for him. A cheapskate. Didn't do drugs. If he held his temper in check, and didn't pull a boss as mean as he was, he might keep a job, get a basement apartment, VCR, live a life of junk food, TV wrestling, Don Cherry tapes, *Hustler* magazine. Crusty kleenex on the coffee table, nudged aside with a dirty socked foot.

That was it—Hrcka could sit in life's crumbs. Travis would die in that world, he knew there was more to it than that. He probably also knew he would never have the chance to find out what it was.

In prison he certainly wouldn't. What a blind and stupid waste. Juve prisons were even worse. You probably wouldn't get killed, but in juve prison there was no resignation yet, no old-timers, no general population settled into the routine. In juve prison, each and every body was at the peak of its hormonal seething. Peak of anger. Hope was cruel because it only complicated things, turning pure and simple anger into despair. Hope had never worked before. Still it twisted invisibly inside, like a sick root. Toughness was the dirt that covered it.

Travis would go there and dig in deep.

Noel closed the car door holding a clutch of corny flowers, and matching her ironic smile greeted Sharon in the kitchen. In that moment of seeing each other, they both knew all that had happened and all that was now being said. They'd never had to talk much.

Still being corny, Noel cupped her neck, bent her back over her heels and kissed her. He pulled her toward the bedroom, but she laughed and ran ahead to pull him faster. They jumped together, landed on the bed. Noel lurched to his knees, growled, fiercely sniffed his armpit like in *A Fish Called Wanda*, an old joke. Smiling while kissing, they undid and wrestled away each other's clothes, something they hadn't done in years, maybe since marriage. He began to nip her throat, her shoulders. She reached down to make him hard but he was already so she was soft with his testicles, to tease. They manoeuvred head to toe to remove each other's socks, and in so doing it was easy, it was necessary, to fall sincere and open their mouths and lick, because there it was. Noel lost his smile as the drive to smile moved down to fire his groin. Their chins worked, gently thrusting, and they grew fevered together, climbing in pace, and Noel was quick to move at

Sharon's nudge that they not finish it this way, no, they moved up eye-to-eye and he entered her exactly as she took him in, and it didn't take them long as they moved faster, gritting their teeth, lips flexed stiff, breath loud, eyes opening wider and wider, and here it came, and as he began to come, as he looked into her eyes, as he fought to keep open the door of vision, he saw what he had always known he would see: two eyes framing a clanging bright emptiness, Sharon nowhere to be seen, space so vast and so clean it was only eyes after all, the fact of blue-green absolute and frightening, the black holes even more.

THE DIVINE RIGHT OF KINGS

THIS TIME MARCIE YELLED FOR A KLEENEX. She yelled again, adding to her order—Roger was to boil some water for her root tea. He could never get the tea's Japanesy name right so they both called it her root tea. She'd brought a big bag of it on vacation, as if she knew she'd be needing it. When anything went wrong with her body, like now, she drank it constantly.

As he would beer. Roger started her root water, then reached into the tiny fridge and removed a cold beer, which he replaced with a warm one from the box. There was room in there for just one, on its side, squishing the lettuce.

As he took a sip, part of him was alarmed that it was only ten in the morning. But it was a medicinal sip, like the hillgranny with her rheumatizz tonic. Medicinal because already, as he sipped, one of his five kids was banging in the screen door to announce boredom and demand the impossible. Medicinal, because the other four would follow with—here they were now, stomping in, they were upon him. Medicinal, because Marcie's back had chosen Prince Edward Island to collapse and keep her in bed, where she could neither enjoy her vacation nor let him enjoy his.

He would sip, no guzzling. Maybe one beer an hour, which, if buffered with occasional food, would dull the edges, the urges to violence, yet allow the watchful eye of a good parent. Little Jess these days toddled at a sprint and had grown a precocious death wish and a hound's nose for the poisonous, the electric. At the other end of the ladder, first-born Ben's sneer told Roger that his thirteen-year-old was on the verge of the sort of trouble that would involve police. The other three, the noisy, fleshy, middle part of the family, were in the transition zone between infantile stupidity and indiscriminate hatred. Roger had sipped it down to empty.

"Sweetheart? Roger? Can—"

"*YES.*"

Her root tea was boiling. He was slicing and handing out greasy coins of garlic sausage, the kids' eyes glazing over and their hands and faces slick with it already.

"Okay. *Outside* with that."

"*What, honey?*"

"*Coming.*"

He caught little Jess by the shoulder, and while she struggled against his hold he licked his thumb and rubbed from her forehead what looked to be dried barbecue sauce. He considered tasting it to check, but didn't.

"*Roger?*"

"*COM—*"

With her cute naughty-game look, Jess had whirled and punched him in the throat.

A reprieve in the guise of an errand, Marcie asked him to go see how Ruby was doing. Letting the screen door squeal and bang behind him, sounding how he felt, Roger heard Marcie begin to read a story-book, could envision the clustered brood. Then shrieks of No! My leg! as someone sat on or wrestled close to her, sending fire up her back. Roger walked faster.

Doctors said take two to start, so Roger had guzzled a couple between trips with her root tea, snack, salt for her snack, not-that-magazine-sorry-the-other-one. As he crossed the lawn to Ruby's, his yeasty rise wasn't as joyful as it was disorienting, given that the sun hadn't yet clanged high noon.

Ruby, the owner of Seaside Farm and Resort, had all week been fretting and lying down a lot, hence Marcie's concern. Ruby's fret involved the imminent arrival of an English lord. Because any actual lord choosing this place was highly unlikely, and because Ruby was ninety-one, none of the other guests paid attention to her flutterings. But as far as Roger and Marcie could see, Ruby was never wrong. She was an energetic, happy, bright, utterly improbable old lady and so Roger figured there might in fact be a lord on his way. But what an image.

Seaside Farm and Resort, as they'd assessed it at first sight, was Hopefully Not Awful. By day three it was Actually Not Bad, mostly in light of it being After all the Cheapest Place on the Island. The tiny cabins were fifty years old and smelled their age, but it was a camp-smell, summery, a bygone sort of mildew. There was a sprawling lawn for children's hysterical, flapping games. A horse to seduce with apples, chickens to chase. Best of all, from a safety point of view, the sea was a five-minute walk, and the beach so gradual that it took another three minutes' hard wading to get deep enough to drown. Marcie and Roger had calculated over beer that, adding in the oxygen factor, they therefore had a twelve-minute grace period before their children suffered any brain damage. And this was if the kids set out to try to drown. So more like fifteen minutes. In any case enough time for two starved parents to crack off a semi-decent one. At this realization, Marcie deemed the place Great. Some levity before her back took her down.

But it wasn't a place a lord would choose. Lord no. No phone, TV, not even radio. Mismatched paint and old amber fly strips. Hotplate. Fridgeen fit for salad makings and a single beer, not the massive roasts and puddings or whatever an English lord would demand for his table.

Roger hoped he and his family weren't part of some noble research on Commonwealth poverty; or some kind of self-betterment experiment, a butlerless camp-out. Or worse, an experiment in slumming. He pictured his swarming family, their dirty faces. Little Jess peeing wherever she happened to be. The father drinking beer at ten in the morning.

He stood at the door of Ruby's big farmhouse, burping quietly. Hoping he didn't smell too much of beer, he rapped and entered. Ruby was country casual. She badgered guests to "drop in, and I mean it." All were invited to "visit the henhouse back of the big house and get your breakfast eggs." Roger and Ben had in fact done this, Ben's sneer faltering in awe of the sign tacked over the chicken-shelves: "Wash your eggs, and leave one for me, Ruby." Ben looked a little scared by it.

Ruby was having a lie-down on the couch.

"Hi there, Ruby."

"Why, hello, Roger. Thanks, I'm just fine."

Hearing was her one sense scuffed by age.

"Any word on the lord?"

"Sorry?"

"ANY WORD ON THE LORD?"

"Oh, why yes, yes." Ruby smiled, a lifting and flowering of wrinkles, but her eyes stayed worried. "His secretary, a man—his secretary is a man!—called from London in England last night to say His Lordship was landing right in Charlottetown this morning. So he's already here." Ruby's smile had slowly been falling, and now it was gone. "The lord is on the island, Roger."

"Well, good. Great."

"Oh dear. I keep—" She stopped breathing.

"Ruby?"

"Why has he picked here? There has to be a mistake."

"He can come to the party tonight. We'll put on a Beatles tape. In his honour." Roger saw she hadn't got his little joke when she looked up at him in fresh panic.

"Oh my. A Beatles? Is that what he—? Do you have one? My grandson could ask around I suppose. A Beatles?"

By late afternoon various guests had done this and that until eventually a few tables were organized in the shade of the big linden tree. A tiny tape deck was stuck to the end of a thick yellow extension cord. Lawn darts and a kite. A beer cooler, at present empty and ajar and holding a purring cat. Passing it by with ashtrays, staggering a little, Roger wondered if his Ben, given this chance, would lock that lid on that cat.

The party was for Ray 'n' Viv, of New Jersey. Exactly thirty years ago they had honeymooned at none other than Seaside Farm and Resort, which, Ray announced in yells, "HASN'T CHANGED A BIT. THANK CHRIST." Ray 'n' Viv were thin, and dressed in identical pastels, parodies of American crass. They were accompanied by their thirty-year-old son, Ray. "HERE WE ARE," Ray Sr. would announce, arm ambushing Jr.'s shoulders, "HERE WE ARE, RAY 'N' RAY." He was also given to pointing to his cabin and stating that little Ray here was likely the result of the honeymoon "there in that cottage, that one you're looking at, CAN YOU BELIEVE IT—RIGHT THROUGH THAT WINDOW." No one, least of all Ray Jr., wanted to picture anything through that window.

Ray Jr. showed public disgust at his father's vulgarity, and spoke to others softly, quickly, and like an intellectual. "Dad—Dad and Mum—*refuse* to experience any other of the island's aspects—any alternatives—there *are* remote spots, tranquil—oddities, not overrun—in any case, *I'm* going."

Dad, eavesdropping from across a lawn, yelled, "So EXPERI-ENCE. GO."

Viv was the most energetic in helping set up her own party, and Roger felt a taint in this. Though, true, the guests were beached-out and tired, and without Viv's help it might not have gotten going at all. But emerging from his cabin, Roger met the unnerving sight of Viv, fiftyish, and Ruby, almost twice that, wrestling an oil-drum bar-becue across the grounds. Both women were covered with rust and soot by the time Roger arrived to help with the final five feet.

Rubber-legged, winded, he set his end down. He had just had an active five minutes with Marcie. Opening a beer in the kitchen, he'd answered another of her calls to find her lying there on the bed, eyeing him dreamily. On her chest was a paperback with a florid, romantic cover. All five children were out raiding the party's potato-chip bowls. Through nothing more verbal than eye contact, Marcie had Roger approach, take down his pants, position himself just so on the bed, and nip-her-neck, the way she loved, while she took him in hand. Roger wondered if this was a reward for his week of suffering service. Or had she just been surprised by a dirty book? Or was this Marcie proving to both of them that, even prone and half-dead, she could turn him into a quivering boy? A minute in, Roger didn't care what her motive was. A minute after that, after he'd exhaled like a dying man and Marcie had given him her naughty-game look and then painfully rolled over for a nap, Roger stood up and zipped up, retrieved his beer from the kitchen, went out to help wrestle the bar-becue, and then witnessed the arrival by taxi of Lord Andrew, Lady Amelia, and their two noblechildren, Kate and Andrew.

He watched poor Ruby shudder at seeing them de-car, watched her suck it up and approach and greet them. She did well, old-fashioned graces coming through as she shook hands and dipped heads. He watched her slip money into the cabby's hand to get him to bring the luggage. It seemed they would be staying in the big house. Roger watched for any lordly reaction to the place, but their glancings around showed only stunned neutrality. They must be, in their lan-guage, frightfully tired.

They made their way to the house. The lord, past middle age, looked like a boy who'd been hopeless at soccer but had been forced to play anyway. He wore his belted pants up over his paunch, like an old nerd. The lady, her hair greasy and hanging, looked half his age. At the moment Roger thought this, she swung her head his way, finding Roger across twenty yards of grass. She met his eye. Hers flashed, and Roger saw that she was beautiful, slyly so. Even after what he'd just been through with Marcie, he felt a stirring. More than that, he saw that she was brilliant, and that he would never have secrets from her.

It turned out that Ray Jr. was a slavering anglophile. He knew all the royals' names, for instance, and was the only man Roger knew who'd watched The Wedding (Roger was unclear which) start to finish. When the lord appeared at eight to join the party, Ray Jr. was on him like mosquitoes, his probings angled and furtive and quick. Seeing his son's interest, Ray Sr. decided to be interested too, but his questions were for the benefit of others, and asked in an extra-rancid voice.

"SO. SO SIR ANDREW." The trace of a smirk, and a hint of quotes around the name. "YOU LIVE IN A CASTLE OR WHAT."

"Just 'Andrew', please." Sir Andrew smiled gently. He looked tentative on his feet, as if they were too tender for this rough land. "Hardly a castle. We have a flat in Chelsea, and we keep a place in Oxford, though—"

"CALL IT WHAT YOU WANT, IT WAS TRAGIC. IT WAS A TRAGEDY. In MY OPINION SHE WAS A LOVELY PERSON."

"One assumes you mean the late Lady D—"

"A REAL HUMAN BEING. I mean, LAND MINES? COME ON."

"Indeed. It was with great—"

"ROUGH TIME FOR THE QUEEN, HUH?"

"Ah. Well, I suppose, yes...." The lord's brows furrowed. Ray Jr. looked as though, had there been a weapon handy, his father would be dead.

"I mean, 'RANDY ANDY'? And, and—THAT FRECKLED ONE, ON THE DIETS? FREDDIE? FERGIE!"

"Yes. Indeed. Indeed."

"YOU EVER, YOU KNOW, TALK TO THE QUEEN ABOUT ALL THAT?" At this, Ray Sr. lurched across the gap between chairs to punch his son's shoulder. Ray Jr., who had decided to die himself, died.

"I am hardly"—the lord had a diplomat's perfect smile—
"what could be termed a *confidant* of Her Majesty. At most, I have
had occasion, during committee work for the House, to consult about
certain, one might say largely 'bureaucratic' matters which—"
        "HOUSE OF LORDS, RIGHT? Jesus, the HOUSE OF
LORDS." Ray smiled at everyone and shook his head.
        Since Ray Jr. was staring off, dead, and not up to it, Roger
considered saying something to shut the bozo up, to show the lord
they weren't all stupid and, more than that, to show him that Canadians weren't as stupid as Americans. Then it dawned on Roger that the
man was simply asking the questions everyone else wanted to ask but
was too scared and sophisticated to.
        "Andrew?" God, Roger was asking the lord a question.
        "Yes?"
        "Care for a beer? I'm on a mission home, refill the cooler."
He jerked a thumb back at his cabin.
        "Ah. Yes, please. Excellent."
        Roger nodded and spun around and away. He felt a surge of
pride. He hadn't sounded either eager or repressed, and the lord had
seemed like a decent guy relieved to have been treated like a decent
guy.
        Marcie was still asleep, so he rattled in the beer quietly. He
filled a bag with one cold, eleven warm Red Dog. Recrossing the lawn
he devised a theory dividing up the Canadians in their response to
this lord. Being Canadian, all were afraid of him, but while one half
avoided him under the guise of aloofness, the other half was so afraid
that, under the guise of bravery, they actually spoke to him. In voices
barely audible they conveyed the most inane sentiments. Bashing Red
Dogs into the ice of the cooler, Roger, proudly a part of neither group,
listened.
        "Sir. Welcome. To PEI."
        "Thank you."
        "Is this, is this your first time to Canada? I, I doubt it, in that
you no doubt travel, a lot, probably.... But, is it?"
        "It's my first visit to this particular province."
        "Ah! And, and...."
        "I like Prince Edward Island very much. Quite scenic."
        "Isn't it though? It *is* a charming island."
        "The brochures were modest."
        Ruby was right, there must have been a mistake. How had

this man with the same honorific as Jesus Christ ended up here? Roger approached him now with two bottles proffered. From the corner of his eye he saw that Lady Amelia had arrived under the linden tree, a child on either side of her.

"Andrew. I have a cold one and a warm one. Your call."

The lord's look was puzzled. Roger tried again.

"It's humble canuck beer but I thought you might like it like at home. Room temp."

"What a splendid label."

"Red Dog."

"I believe I'll opt for the chilled. Do as the natives, and all that."

Roger handed him the cold one. The warm one felt suddenly warmer in his hand. This one he would definitely sip. Was the wife, the Lady, smiling at him? Yes, but it was her eyes, just her eyes doing the smiling. She was a foxy one. Bit of a looker. "Looker", Jesus. A few minutes with these people and here he was talking Brit.

The lord was again stalled. Someone had handed him a mug, and he stood helplessly eyeing it and the unopened beer.

"Twist top," Roger said. He demonstrated on the wet mouth of his own half-empty bottle.

Lord Andrew regarded the Red Dog with suspicion, then with adventure. He took a firm grip, actually took a breath, and twisted. At the bottle's hissy burp he visibly startled, and announced, "Oh dear!"

He poured the beer proudly, glugging it in from straight over top until he had one inch of beer and seven of foam, and a soaked hand. To all this he said, "Good head." His eyes had the determined but vacant look of a man who makes no mistakes.

And here Roger witnessed a gesture he instantly recognized to be foreign to this country. What the lord did with his emptied bottle was hold it out to his side, tilted at an expectant angle, positioned for a servant's removal. Here the bottle hung, waiting, servants an ocean away. Perturbed at this negligence, Lord Andrew gave the bottle a little waggle. Roger stood spellbound. The waggle was bored and impatient and habitual, not unlike Cinderella's stepmother's bellwork. When the lord awoke to where he was, he had another little startle and then, all by himself, placed the bottle on the picnic table. Lord Ordinary. Lord of White Pudding. Roger wondered if the "divine right of kings" had ever and in any way applied to lords as well, a blue blood trickle-down. But he had decided to like Lord Andrew, above the cheap affection given novelties. The man was gentle, and meant well. An innocent. An old lamb. Odd how the worldly can be of a different world than the actual. And the party already seemed to be turning away from him, growing louder around him while not including him, a cage of crude noise. Hysterical with relief that her poor resort had survived royalty, Ruby bounced on the spot like an ancient girl. Ray Sr., fighting everyone's noise and winning, shouted the details of the seduction that had led to Jr.'s conception. He had hold of his wife's wrist, thrusting it at the lord to show the size of her wedding ring, which according to his yells had had lots to do with her carnal swoon.

Roger found himself approaching Lady Amelia. She sat at the end of a bench at the party's farthest edge. Her attendance looked dutiful, in that English way. At her flanks, her children sat in a virtual stupor of duty, bug-eyed with fatigue, head-thick with lag.

"Get you something to drink?" Of all the guests he'd been here longest and it was natural to play host. He had caught himself on the verge of saying, Can I be of service.

"A brandy or something? A scotch?" Her smile was almost too lovely.

"Have to ask Ruby if she has anything like that. I was offering, I guess, your basic beer, or beer." He nodded to the kids. "Or lemonade."

"Three lemonades would be perfect." She dipped down to whisper something about "lemon squash" to her children, who weren't at all moved by the news.

"I could ask Ruby about the brandy." Already into the mission, he looked up for the old lady.

"No, it's—"

Both of them were suddenly laughing, having located Ruby in the crowd, plunging her face into the chip bowl and taking one up on her tongue, possibly demonstrating to the children how a great blue heron stabs a fish. She pointed her face at the moon and gulped the chip down. Roger and Lady Amelia shared an "isn't life absurd and wonderful" look.

"No, I shouldn't. I'm just here for the moment. Lemon is my ticket tonight." She looked at him marvelling over what she had just said. "I'm Amelia by the way."

"Amelia." He felt his tongue's liquid dance. Amelia Bye the

Waye. He shook her hand. A give of bones in flesh.

"And you're?"

"'Lady Amelia'...."

"No, that's me."

"No, I know. Sorry. Roger."

"Hello. Roger."

She said his name as he pivoted for the lemon squash, and though she said it nicely enough it sounded to his ears like the name of a wide-faced serf who lived in his own shit a mile's trudge from the manor. He found three plastic cups, one of them used (that would be for one of the kids), and tried not to spill the lemonade he poured, pausing to finger a dead bug from one (the other kid's). He was tired and drunk and knew he was in deep danger. He hadn't been so instantly afraid of a woman since high school, and that woman was lying on her bad back in a cabin fifty yards away.

With one of his middle-children whining and clamped to his leg, trying to go to sleep on it, Roger delivered the drinks. Amelia's eyes, thanking him under the fragrant linden tree, were almost unbearable. Her mouth offered a wry little smile that could have meant— everything. Shall we do it, slowly, now, on the beach? You have a child on your leg. Lemon squash, how nice, do you love me?

Looking at her, Roger felt on the verge of some sort of idiocy when, luckily, Ray Sr. roared up for introductions. He had a humiliated but excited Jr. by the arm.

As practised as Andrew, Amelia was gracious. When Ray Sr. learned that her young lad was also an Andrew—that is, a Jr.—he shouted at the stricken boy, "ANDREW TWO! ANDY THE SECOND! ANDY JUNIOR! ALL RIGHT!" and ran off to claim kinship with the lord.

"I have to—I want to apologize—for Dad." The Jr. Ray was on her. "He doesn't understand how to—he doesn't, he doesn't respect proper distance."

"Your father is an absolute blast, don't be silly."

"Mummy?" Young Andrew, about eight, looked near tears. "Mummy? May we go up now?"

"He doesn't—as your people might say—know his place."

"Oh nonsense. He's fine." Her lovely smile fixing all. Roger could see in her eyes her accurate assessment of Jr. Ray, that here was a thirty-year-old on a sulking vacation with his parents.

"Mummy?" Little Andrew's voice was Christopher Robin's.

"You could stay, Mummy. I could go alone. I could read my new book."

"Ah—the young lord." Ray Jr. swivelled his hunger to the boy and stooped to reverently shake his hand. "How do you do—Sir."

"I am not a lord. My father is a lord."

"Ah—but you will be—one day."

"When my father dies." The boy's look turned severe, and his lower lip began to tremble.

"That's right!—and on that day—you will ascend—with all rights and privileges—to the House of—"

"Andrew, let's be off, your book is a good idea." Amelia stood, putting her shoulder into Ray Jr.'s chest. "I have a book too. Kate, come along, bring your squash."

With that, she made off with her children, leaving Roger and Ray Jr. staring after her.

"Long flight," Roger suggested.

"She's a—bitch." Ray's look was that of the newly hatched traitor.

At the porch, the lemon-light of the wrought-iron lamp suggesting mist, Amelia swung her face over her shoulder. "Thank you, Roger."

Ra-jah. Roger closed his eyes. Amelia could save him. Ra-jahhh. His own name sounded like the very breath of elegant sex. She could save him from all this. The middle-child had fallen asleep at his feet, arms limp around his ankle.

He gathered his brood to take home to bed. This took an hour and several beer and much shouting and violent wrestlings-to-the-grass. Son Ben had beer on his breath, little Jess candle wax in her hair, and one of the middle ones was wearing someone else's clothes. It had begun to rain.

Job done, veering past Marcie's bedroom door, Roger was beckoned. Marcie had a new book folded on her lap. Eyeing it, Roger stumbled. But all she had for him was a little speech. It was heavy-handed and clear. She knew his state.

"Roger. You don't remember this. We promised Ruby a clambake before we left. Tomorrow's our last day, so tomorrow we dig clams. Low tide is in the morning. If you can walk—"

"What y'mean fie can walk?"

"—if you can walk, go invite the lord and lady to dig with us. They'll love it. Don't argue."

"They're bloody asleep." Jesus, an English accent.

"Their light's on." Marcie pointed out her window at the big house. So from her cell she had been keeping tabs, and had her own version of things.

Before he knew what was what, knowing only that he must not think anything at all, he'd passed Ruby asleep on her couch and was knocking on their door, Her door. And good God here she was, framed in doorway light. Smiling yet professionally unsurprised, as if expecting something, something "raucous". He thought of the words, Naughty Victorian.

"Hello. 'Roger,' wasn't it?"

"Hi, jus' wanted to mention the party."

"The, the party?"

Pah-ty. Lovely. Speak some more. He waited. Victorians like her—their floor-length frills and scented rooms and chamber music and life one big happy euphemism—thought of absolutely nothing except hard sex. He didn't want to think ill of her, this Lady Amelia here, because she was friendly, and funny, and wise, all of those, but you couldn't help but look at her, and then at poor old Andrew, pale and paunchy and sixty, a gormless lord. She was probably good to him, but come on. There was no way you could look at her and see "Lady Amelia". She should be someone called Lisette, Lisette Barker, the dangerous one in your grade eleven class, Lisette who you lusted after in fear until one night, both of you drunk at a party, you fall into each other's arms, you can't believe your luck, but you're up to the task, Lord Jesus yes you are, your time is steamy and thick and your moans are broken only by laughter incredulous in the discovery that pleasure can be so pleasant. Lisette Barker. You are too tame for her fire and after a month she dumps you, and five months after that she's married to a criminal.

"Hello?" Lady Amelia was hunching to peer into Roger's stare. "Are we, are we done?"

"Clams."

"Excuse me?"

"Clam digging. Clams for the party, the one tomorrow night."

"Ah, another party. And clamming?"

"No, the clamming's during the day. To get clams for the party. Clambake. Old-fashioned, for Ruby. We thought maybe your kids, your children, or maybe even you yourself, might like to—" Roger came back into his brain, and smiled. "—to slog around in some mud with us, forage for molluscs."

"Lady Amelia" laughed beautifully. "I haven't had an invitation like that in ages. Lord Andrew and I and the children would be most delighted." May-ost de-lahted. God, she was mocking herself. He loved her. She wasn't a gold-digger. He was ashamed of himself. Desperately poor, she had had to marry the dull noble in order to pay off her parents' medical bills.

Despite the drawing-room acceptance her look was wryly confidential, sexually bittersweet. Her eyes flashed a metallic lustre, a kind of makeup you couldn't buy.

"Another party. My word." Pah-ty. She looked in no hurry to leave her door sill.

"It's all we do here. Canada."

He wanted to lean in, touch his cheek to hers and close his eyes. She could save him, and he could save her. Look at her, feverish with dreams of escape. This golden cage.

"Well, splendid. And the clamming."

"Good. Low tide's at, I'll check. Ruby has pails and shovels in the barn. The smaller one. The one behind the, you know, the bigger one. Barn."

"Fine. Are you all right to drive?"

"I'm not dr— I'm staying with you, I mean here. In one of the...." He saw her smile. God, she was a wily one. Lady Sardonic. His stagger had been so small he'd hardly noticed it himself. "Got me."

"Gotcha. Good-night then, Roger." She smiled again, not yet turning into her room, royal euphemism all over her face. Roger looked past her at the bed in there, no lord in it. Was he asleep somewhere else? Did they have two rooms?

Recognizing certain death when he saw it, he turned away first.

"Night. 'Amelia'."

Even asleep he knew the day was too bright. He suffered a morning dream that Marcie was bravely out of bed and had a weird hat on, a bonnet. He awoke in the middle of a sincere moan, passing out again when the moan ran out of breath. His waking continued on and off like this for an hour, when several children were sent in to jump on him, shouting, "*Clams!*"

His only clean shirt, the one he'd avoided up till now, was very white and orange, brighter than the day, and hurt to wear. Marcie was in fact up, and she did have a ball cap on her head. From the side of his face Roger witnessed his children eating a breakfast of potato chips and butter. He heard them leave for the beach, dragging shovels on the road behind them, loud but too slow for sparks. He could smell the low tide that waited for him out there. He knew he would soon be in the middle of that smell, digging up the little meat pouches that created it.

Head in hands, elbows on table, he teetered over his coffee. A walk, the beach. Gravelly sucking shovel sounds under the hot sun. Why did he find himself thinking of Malcolm Lowry, the Brit who drank and wrote here and then went home to England to die? Wait— England, Canada, last night, the Lord. The Lady. Amelia.

He rose shaking, Lowry-like, feebly trusting that in action, in walking, his pain would fade to the background. He got outside, but the pain simply grew bigger than the day. Walking felt like flying, in that he might go down. He squinted past tourists and villagers, he suffered the mixed aroma of coconut oil and manure. He didn't know why, but it was important that he arrive before her, that he have at least a half pail of clams before she got there. He pictured himself bent over her—the clamless lord looking on—bent over her, showing her how to dig.

The simple vista of sea and sky—two blues meeting in the middle of his vision, bisecting it cleanly—did ease his pain. As did the breeze on his face. What hurt was the crowd out there on the flats. Scattered on the hard sand, hunting the area at their feet, intense even at this distance. They looked like Dali's version of farmers, addled lost naked farmers, working a dead, timeless, skin-bald field.

They were all here. All of them. Marcie. His children. Old Ruby. Ray 'n' Ray 'n' Viv. The lord, Lord Nothing, and his two Pooh kids. And Her. The Lady. Lady Much. She who knew him to his depths. She who would save him. Was she reading his thoughts even now? Soothing them? This breeze on his face was from her.

He arrived in their midst in the middle of a vague argument, and it looked as if its two main participants were, good God, Amelia and Marcie. They were digging side by side.

"It's *not* that they look frightful, though they do. It's that they'll go *bad.*" Lady Amelia bent and tugged a fleshy bullet from the hole at her feet and plopped it into her half-full pail.

"Not in an hour or two," Marcie said. "Just keep them under a bit of water." Marcie finished a hole but, careful of her back, pointed down and little Jess ran in to grab the clam. She dropped it into her mom's pail, singing "Boop!" as it hit.

"Well *we* won't be eating them, I shouldn't think."

It was odd but her voice sounded different, pinched, no throaty lustre. Perhaps it was all this sunlight.

The genteel fight had to do with damaged clams. It seemed that Amelia had been leaving any shovel-broken clams by the wayside, and Marcie had been disturbed by the waste, the needless killing. At her request, son Ben was retracing their path with a bucket, picking them up. Roger could hear him moaning, "Bring out yer dead. Bring out yer dead."

He knew he was staring at her. Amazing how clothing could keep a body secret. Lady Amelia's wasn't a "bad" body. Of course it wasn't. But it was a weird body. And no doubt surprise made it seem weirder than it probably actually was. But her pelvis was a bulb, as wide front-to-back as it was hip-to-hip. A machined pearness. Her limbs were perfectly tubular, with no hint of muscle. The effect was that she looked like a big, unformed, unused baby. But what was this to-do about bodies anyway? Here at middle age, spirit and desire could do the trick.

Neither woman had seen him yet. They were discussing bivalve nervous systems, Amelia saying that compassion for clams was absurd, they had no feeling whatever, they had shells for godsake, and Marcie suggesting that since we didn't know for sure how it felt to be a clam, to be on the safe side we shouldn't unthinkingly torture them.

In fear of being made to comment, Roger turned away, but Marcie saw him.

"Speaking of nervous systems, it's ROGER-DODGER!"

Right at him, as loud as she could. Marcie could be such a teenager.

His hand involuntarily cupping the side of his head, he tried not to squint as he talked, as he whispered.

"You're up. How's the back?"

"I bored it to death." His wife laughed, reckless, fresh, indeed like a teenager. "I don't care any more. I wanted to be here."

Jess ran in for a new clam when her mother pointed, and Roger thought he saw Marcie wince to move her arm. Marcie in her baseball cap. He liked her in that cap.

"Good morning, Roger." Ra-jah. "Have we recovered?"

"Hi. No." An awkward pause. "How are you and yours?"

"Just *mahv*elous. Ruby gave us our breakfast, which was nice indeed, a *lovely* breakfast, just wonderful, and it's so very nice out today. *Lovely. Very* nice indeed."

"Well. Good."

She met his eye but her look was nothing but a nice-breakfast look. How was it that her baby-body made her words seem unwise as well? Her flesh looked pale, newly freed. Clammy. She still hadn't washed her hair—the European influence? Hair like strips of greased metal had a way of accentuating the wide babyishness of things.

"It *is* quite, I don't know, *won*derful here. When we return from the beach I really *do* think I'm going to write a postcard to my sister all about how nice Canada is. Because really it's all quite lovely indeed." She smiled off into this lovely near future, apparently believing in it.

Roger stood looking at her. Who was this woman?

"Lucky you don't feel worse," Marcie said to him, perhaps misreading his face. "Amelia was telling me Andrew went on a bit of a rampage last night. Got into some Canadian Club with Ray."

"Andrew *so* wanted to fetch you out of bed but I wouldn't let him," Amelia added.

"Ray has a headache." Marcie nodded at the silent figure leaning on his shovel, breathing hard for no apparent reason. Nearby, Ray Jr. strolled with his mother, hand in hand. "But His Lordship," Marcie nodded in another direction, "seems okay."

"Odd how he manages," said Amelia. "I don't know that he slept at all." She gazed off at him, looking blandly worried. "He does enjoy his vacations."

At water's edge, Lord Andrew was briskly striding through flat tongues of surf. Now he turned their way. He looked almost rakish in his straw hat, his sleeveless jean vest, his white cotton pants rolled to the knees. Quite alone, he was laughing, a booming laugh. Roger saw that he had a cell phone at his ear. As he neared them they could hear his voice, rich and eager.

"I do wish he'd do some clamming," said Lady Amelia, petulant but cowardly.

Roger removed his gaze from her flesh when he found himself thinking of wind-dried porridge. He looked out to sea. He considered lifting a shovel. The lord's exclamations joined the stew of his consciousness: "...get out of it, man! ...that's fantastic!... I'm phoning Bob! Well yes, I am...I'm phoning Bob!"

Roger smelled the sun on Marcie's skin before he felt her touch. She leaned a cocked elbow on his shoulder, supporting herself on him, careful to keep her wet and gritty hands away. One leg touched his along its entire length.

"How's your head?" Her voice soft, penetrating his mess.

"I'll live." He took another breath, as if testing this theory.

"Back's a bit better?"

"A bit. I'm fine."

"That's great." It did make him feel lighter, this news, even though she was leaning harder on him.

"If we go around stuck together like this," Marcie smiled lazily, "me the head, you the body, neither of us will be a burden on society."

"Right."

As if on cue, little Jess joined them, literally, by sitting on Roger's foot and wrapping her arms around both their legs.

"Walk!" she commanded.

The lord had been dialling and talking to an operator, and Roger caught the words "*North* Vancouver. Yes." He was twenty feet away, still walking toward them, his ear to the phone, grinning in mischief and anticipation. He didn't look like a man who hadn't slept.

"Bob? Bob!... Yes!... Actually, Prince Edward Island!... Bob, listen!... Gino astral projected!... No!... Yes!... Well that's what he said!"

Lord Andrew marched past them and kept going, acknowledging no one. They watched him, heads turning in unison as he passed.

"Well I know.... Well of course.... Well who isn't dreaming, you silly fucker! That's what it's about!... Right. Well of course. Ah, good show. Do call him, yes."

They watched him walk away. He stomped through a tide pool like a child doing a puddle. They could hear his laughter, but no longer his words.

"Andrew has this, he has this pack of *friends*," Amelia was saying, a sudden frenzy of apology. "It's more like, more like a sort of *club*. Spread out all over. I don't much like them, I truly don't."

But Roger and Marcie had turned away from her, had been dragged away, actually, as another child joined the family sculpture, pulling on it until it began to move jerkily along the sand. A further child leapt aboard Roger's other leg, and then another clutched his waist. They made a grotesquely tall and impractical crab, spastically skittling, threatening to topple. They all screamed as they did fall at Ben's casual push, good son Ben who held his mother firm and safe while pushing the rest of them down. Ben and mother stood regarding the squirming pile, Ben looking down in dire judgement of his father.

"Think he'll fit in here?" Ben asked his mother, holding up the pail of wounded clams.

One of the middle ones joined the judgement, yelling, "Dog-pile on Daddy!"

The heap of children shifted its purpose and its mass, climbing up onto their father. They twisted and wrestled and punched and shrieked reptilian, and Ben joined in, and so did Marcie with a foot, working gritty toes beneath his waistband, and Roger was screaming louder than all of them, sand chafing his skin, little hands pummelling his pain away, beating him out of himself, saving him once again.

WITH YOUR HAND IN SATAN'S GLEAMING GUTS

My acquaintance has instructed that, in order to solicit help in a mission that is at once moral and profound, it would be best if I simply told my story:

I believe it started in the summer of 1984, at a lakeside cottage of a colleague from work. Though it rained all weekend, the five of us fellows had quality time. Walks along the narrow beach, games of bridge while the odd man out prepared the next meal. An occasional glass of homemade ale, conversations into the night. I don't recall that my deed was connected to any awareness of the date—that is, 1984, Orwell's book and what it entailed—though in some sense my actions did, and do, meet that book's thematic intention. Perhaps it was in the air that someone begin. Perhaps I was, am, just a willing minion of time's profound and moral arrow.

But it was a pivotal point in my life and I remember it clearly. We arrived late of a Friday evening. By the time we'd unpacked and settled and had something of a chat out on the lawn, gazing across the ebon lake, it was almost time for bed. What one fellow, Robert—or Bob, as he liked being called—what Robert had said disturbed me. Eyeing the TV set as we arrived, he had uttered various enthusiasms about some televised sport taking place tomorrow. Other of the men had grunted back their awareness of the event. Golf, baseball, it was one of those. I was careful not to say a word for fear of what my voice might betray. I was so alive with the thought that some of these men, whom I didn't well know, might after this weekend be my friends, and Robert had made me fearful. I could not bear the image of us fronting a TV all the weekend long—arguing hitting averages or holes-in-one or what athlete had been bought by what team—and me with not a word to say. Standing there under the moon, hearing Robert moan about the big vicarious game tomorrow, I wanted to blurt something to the effect of "Does no one else see irony in driving three hours to a natural paradise in order to watch TV?" But I held back. In casual male society the lazy voice of sports easily defeats the profound.

In any case, I was inspired by the mouse turds. (There are rewards to keeping one's eyes open, and in this lies the essence of my mission.) Above my bed, on a shelf holding some books, I noticed a nibbled book cover and some droppings. Seeing the turds I enjoyed a brief eureka response. Then I went looking for a sharp knife.

The TV waited in the living-room. It was delicious that it was Robert asleep on the sofa-bed not ten feet from where I set to work. I'd put masking tape over the flashlight face, halving its light, amazed at my cunning as each new angle of subterfuge revealed itself to me. I knew I couldn't just cut the cord—it would be repaired in minutes. No, instead I became a mouse, a rat, expertly eating away. I chipped at the cord with my knife, leaving nibbly bits ascatter and a beaverish pattern of hungry nicks where it was fatally severed. I had no idea if a mouse or rat could bite through copper wire; I would leave that mystery to the others. Nor did I know if any rodent would spirit away a severed piece of cord and its plug, though there is the term "pack rat". My final bit of foxiness was to bring some turds from my room and deposit them at the damage site.

One evolves in a new career by making mistakes. Freedom from error likely indicates both blind luck and also, ironically, a dangerous lack of learning. In any case, we had a wonderful weekend. As I mentioned, we conversed and we walked and we lifted our city-drained faces to nature for a shy but thirsty look. So my little crime had served us. Flushed with pride at this, I made my mistake, emerging from my room just as we were about to start the drive back, holding the severed cord aloft and saying something like "Look what I seem to have found!" I've never been a good actor. Or perhaps what gave me away were my several near-speeches about the evils of TV and our serendipitous freedom from it. I was likely shaking a little, excited at the prospect that even as they were discovering my crime, they were recognizing the clear benefit of what I had done and were forgiving if not thanking me. Well, this wasn't the case. I realized I'd made a mistake when the car ride back was distinctly quieter than the one coming, and no one engaged me directly.

My mistake was in the revealing, not the doing. Let me be

clear on this. Quite simply, people do not like to be told when they have been saved. Since that first time, I no longer tell. (I am telling you, true enough. But my acquaintance agrees that my presumptions of mutual trust and respect are likely well founded. In a nutshell, the fact that you are at this moment reading means that you are my ally. So much so that I can relate to you my stylistic quandary in the composing of this: I've felt the occasional urge not only to use short, dramatic, rhetorical structures, but also to paragraph by way of leaving two-line gaps in the text. That is, I've been tempted to seduce readers by using both the sound and the visual bite. Namely, the tools of the screen. I've resisted!)

I did, though, come close to telling Sensei. A moral and profound man, he would never turn me in. I have no doubt of this. I consider him the human being closest to my heart. That we have never met outside the dojo and have spoken only of aikido (and once the weather, when I arrived wet) means nothing. When he throws me and I roll perfectly to complete his intention, the look of love in his eyes is clear. When he counters my feeble attempt at a throw and laughs, I believe it is the laugh of a friend, and several times I have taken the bold step of laughing too. In any case, his insistence that each new student divulge his reasons for wanting to learn this martial art almost elicited my complete confession. "Sensei," I almost blurted that first day, in love with him already, "Sensei, to save others I break into their homes and when I do this I am at times surprised and attacked."

I didn't tell him because simply to say I break into houses would very much misrepresent my mission. And to have launched into an explanation of my pure intention would have burdened Sensei with details. I could see right away—as I stood answerless and he had already interrupted two other beginners in their stumbling explanations—that he was not a man of this petty world, and had little time for the mere crust that is language.

But had I told, I would have explained that I had no choice but to break and enter, that simply cutting an outside cable or knocking over an antenna no longer worked—people merely assumed teenaged vandals and, after they missed an evening of TV (too angry, too caught up in what seemed an unbearable emergency to realize that their lives were suddenly better), their cables and antennas were easily repaired. And in their hunkering down in front of their reborn sets I could feel their urgency and determination to watch TV as never before, their eyes' hard sucking at the picture reminding me of a feeding infant whose panic is over because the teat that had slipped away is back. So simplistic destruction backfired. But I learned as a result. I learned that I had to get right in, there in the belly of the beast, and do more subtle work.

My first two proper jobs involved family gatherings—one a wedding, one a reunion—and I will take credit for the success of both. On both occasions I had opportunity to remove the TVs' cowl and do proper damage. By proper I mean incomplete, partial. (The profound parallel between my work and aikido should surprise no one. As Sensei uses an opponent's own *chi* to defeat him, so I use television's electricity.) I won't go into technical details, not because I don't trust you but because the information is arcane and best left for those of you who want to go farther. Suffice to say that the introduction of an inappropriate metal somewhere in the copper feed will create a partial blockage of the signal. There are methods of creating periodic, progressive snow, or a darkening tube, or a horizontal flip every twelve seconds—any number of irritations that, like the many chronic human ailments that are hard to put a diagnostic finger on, make TV life not quite worth living. Reception so bad that even the most resolute hockey supporter can last no more than five minutes because he cannot distinguish Gresky the Great from Mario the Superman no matter how hard he (or she!) claims the contrary.

A partial, creeping destruction is far better because viewers stricken with a sick rather than a dead set will tend to wait before sending it out for repair. They will huddle around their ailing unit, they will murmur little pleas for it to get well in time for the next show. They will jiggle the cable, bang the set gently on the side, turn it on and off; some, remembering the days of flooded carburettors, will shut it off and let it sit a few minutes and then try again. They may call their cable company and listen to the busy signal awhile. Then they will leave it overnight, hoping for magic.

In the meantime they will find something else to do.

I wonder how many children have made up new games because of me? How many friendships begun or revived? How many ageing couples have relearned rummy or whist, or the art of conversation? And by removing the glaring one-eyed chaperone, I wonder how many babies I have had a hand in conceiving?

Of course—my idealism is not naive—I also have instigated

marital spats, sibling disputes, crushing boredom. All of that. Perhaps
I have angled more than a few couples towards divorce because they
had to talk again and flounder in a chasm of miscommunication, the
discovery of which until now had been avoided by a push on the zapper;
perhaps I've even nudged some of the more hopelessly TV-addicted
into suicide, I don't know. But hardship is a part of life, a part of
living, and as such it too is a part of my mission.
Not everyone's salvation feels the same.

You may have already drawn comparisons between myself and the
Unabomber. We both chose a destructive route, and now we both
have communicated our motivations in print. This comparison is un-
derstandable but wrong. One, the degree of violence. Two, the place
of publication. (I am not being funny when I say that the Unabomber
probably once watched too much television.)

My acquaintance has assured me that the organ in which
this will likely appear will cater to a segment of the population that is
literary, perhaps even in a rarefied sense, and is therefore not likely to
turn me in due to some frenzy of hallucination born of an addictive
allegiance to TV. That is, he's assured me of a readership willing,
through its complicit silence, to enter into what amounts to a criminal conspiracy.

Let me add that I am, as they say, no spring chicken. I have
no biological sons. So in this public passing of the torch I trust I have
adopted sons not only literary but, by extension, moral and profound.

I know I needn't preach. Must I even go into reasons? For
they are known to you. The decline in children's creativity. Our shrinking attention span. Our loss of rhetorical dexterity, our shift from
complex syntax to the bite—Jamesian eloquence defeated in discourse's
back alley by Stallone's grunted near-witticism. I could go on, and
render us all depressed: when not only our entertainment but the val-
ues that feed and shape our souls are being delivered by the electric
agent of Nike, might we not ask if someone shouldn't simply push the
Button and have done with this once noble experiment called hu-
manity?

I sense that we, as dupes of Chaos, are becoming little more
than history's spillage.

Do the poor understand how inexpensive their food would
be if an ageing movie star hadn't been hired to hold the can up to the

camera and tell them that they should eat it?

Do we now have to travel to the hills of the rural Orient to happen upon a father teaching his son how to fly a kite? Strolling a new neighbourhood, looking into windows and their death-blue flicker, I think of the sad irony of the notion of "living-room" and it makes me cry. It's true: I have cried, and I admit this without shame or fear of emasculation in your understanding eyes.

I shouldn't go on, but it galls me how TV leads us whites to believe that all Negroes are Bill Cosby professionals or rich rap singers or athletes. Our Negro brothers not only don't die of AIDS, they come back and resume their sports careers. If I were a moral and profound Negro, I'd heave my TV out the window.

I am not one of those zealots who claim that TV causes cancer or other physiological disease. But so what if TV did cause cancer? What would be the difference? A mindless zombie is a mindless zombie, whether or not he has a tumour or two leeching away in his mindless meat.

I won't go on, but I have seen a woman with a terminal illness, with four months to live, sit out her precious remaining nights in front of her TV, the lights out, the screen-glow lighting up her face, a gothic scenario if ever there was. People would visit, attempt to engage her in card games or friendly talk, and you could see how hard it was for her to tear her gaze away from drivel, from sitcoms she didn't even particularly like. It was the most depressing thing I have ever witnessed. My mother died one day shy of the predicted four months.

What I have come to call my mission began only after long periods of trial. I learned how to "case" a neighbourhood, I took on the education of the apprentice thief. I won't enter into a political theme at this point, but the advent of dual-career couples striving for purchasing power as prompted by TV culture makes for countless empty houses during work hours and an easier career for me.

I recall my first true break-in. I had done the homes and TVs of relatives, acquaintances, those people in my neighbourhood whose habits were known to me. (That summer it wasn't the work of my imagination that there were more children outside playing and more adults astroll. The Autumn Block Party and Corn Boil was reborn after a decade's lapse and only I, and now you, know why.)

But my first time entering a house whose owners were

utterly unknown to me proved an unexpected delight. Putting my head through the jimmied window, I breathed air most enlivening— dark, cool, oxygen-rich. Danger, I learned, as have countless explorers before me, makes one's senses leap to the fore and makes life's mundane offerings stand out as though in bas-relief. Colours, smells, and textures hoist one to an experiential paradigm the likes of which I imagine was habituated by Blake, de Quincey, Rimbaud, and, it seems, Dante.

I don't recall when it was I decided to start taking a wage. That is, money for labour. Perhaps the notion took root that this was my new "job"; and, moreover, that good works demand and deserve remuneration. Also, travel seemed a necessary next step—not only had my rash of good deeds been noted in the local newspaper, but it dawned on me that the Sherwood Forest of television was vast, and virgin.

But never, never for profit. I don't think I've taken more than a thousand dollars' worth of cash or goods from any one home. My needs remain spartan. My car is an economical Toyota, renewed every eighteen months, and its only option air conditioning, this seeming luxury an adjunct of my often working an urban area during the muggy depths of summer while its residents are slightly north watching TV in their cottages. I generally patronize a modest Travelodge or Super 8. Any place with a half-decent TV.

Yes, TV. Let me explain. In my room, resting between jobs, I lie back and turn on the TV set. I do. I do because it will make my next job so much the easier, so much the easier for the bile that rises as I zap through the insipid flickerings that poison us all. Soon I am sitting up straight as I watch, feeling the rancid image enter and infect not only my mind but my body; like a bodhisattva I invite it and absorb it because in so doing I suffer for the sake of all beings. And when the fleshy likes of "Friends" comes on, or "Baywatch", I rise to this worst of all offerings, I stand close to the TV and watch, hard, this scourge of titillation, this agony of sexual promise unfulfilled, I watch again and again and more and, come the end, come the end oh, I rely on shame, and then the rage, once more to get me out the door and on my mission....

In any case, I suspect several hotel chains are becoming suspicious of a repeat customer whose visits coincide with the somewhat spectacular (allow me this immodesty) aberration of yet another of their TV sets displaying its picture upside-down.

It's possible that you yourself have benefited from my work. If you suspect you have, ask yourself: did it truly hurt? After a mere moment's irritation, was your life not made better? Perhaps you took up reading again. It is possible that, without my hand in your life, you would not be reading this.

I'm beginning to have a problem with the Internet. How about you? Defenders tell me it involves reading, but does it? Does it really? A prose style born of board games and want ads! The hiccupping syntax! Fragments in neon! Sexual enticements dangled like bait!

I am aware that you may have even stronger feelings than mine on these matters. You may be among those who feel that behind TV's onslaught is an organized conspiracy, a corporate dictatorship whose master plan is to enslave the populace by making them drink this cola, buy that shoe, maintain this status quo, adopt that way of life. And they are so smart that they even let us little people make our own dribbles of TV—not only PBS, but America's Funniest Videos, those reels of violent pap and amateur flatulence. But, no, there is no conspiracy. In fact, I believe that those who hold this view are paranoid and (again I am not being funny) have been watching too much TV.

The human race is not smart enough to coordinate such a thing. I wish it were. Because what is actually taking place is far worse.

I propose an equation for you who favour logic. (Let me add that, though I have training in formal rhetoric, and though I admit to appealing to both reason and emotion here, my intentions are as inviolate, as selfless, as language itself.) I propose: if Jesus Christ represents pure love, then Satan is by definition pure hate. Correct? That is one view of things Christian. Another, perhaps more subtle: if God is pure intelligence, perfect mind, then is not Satan perfect non-mind? Further, if God is the richest message possible, that is, absolute content, then the opposite is absolute non-content, an utter dearth of message altogether. By definition then, Satan is that which would occupy us completely, and *occupy us with absolutely nothing*.

The medium is indeed the message—*but there isn't one.* We wait, watching, imprisoned within a bestial vacuum, a horned bell jar. (Those were not rabbit ears, fools.)

It is already happening. You do know this.

Listen: the first time I removed the matte-black TV cowl, exposing the butt of the tube and the thick, ripe, sensate cable entering it like an evil umbilicus—feeding the TV's anus, which is appropriate—I encountered amid the set's organs a bundle of multicoloured wires. I placed my hand upon them. And in the cool dark of sanctity, breathing the pure air of the holy thief, I gave a gentle tug. My heart began to beat, a noble drum urging me in the rightness of my task. With my hand in Satan's gleaming guts I pulled harder, and then harder, and as the wires began to squeal and pop I knew that I was ripping out the life of Nike, and professional sports, and Exxon, and sexual promise unfulfilled, and Nite News from Detroit, and psychic hotlines, and Abflex, and televangelism, and Gulf Wars to come, and the frightening frightening advertising that's getting stronger than holy will itself. I knew as I pulled that I was also pulling out those few moral PBS shows—but I knew as well that this seeming impurity in my mission would be redeemed by those who, free now, would rise up and go out-of-doors to encounter the PBS issues in the flesh. They'd smell the real air and realize that the smokestacks belching behind glass were not nearly so profound as this.

So, please. Imagine, on the sacred screen of your mind: you are looming over a TV set, lifting a screwdriver. Deftly you remove the black shell; you ease your hand into the blind intestines of evil, and then you are ripping them out, you are ripping and snuffing the flow of their toxic electric blood, you can hear and see the tube die and you can feel the blessed *living-room* released at last. The very air expands in silence and profundity both. You can sense the flexing wings of a vast unseen dove. You can see, for you still know how to see, the sunlight penetrate the window and place a holy square on the floor at your feet. The square has heat, and a smell, and it is brilliant. It has been sent from millions of miles away and it is as close to communication as we can come.

Dug

SMILING, COY IN A WAY THAT MOCKED ITSELF, June whispered that she
wanted to take a shower first.

Robert sat waiting on her couch and she was in there now
showering away. It was something like in the movies, how you could
hear the faint spray and snatches of her humming. It felt strange, a
little vertiginous, knowing that in minutes he would be in the middle
of sex.

He thumbed a women's magazine. All the fine bodies in the
ads, so young and looking somehow savage for it. In minutes he and
June would be seeing each other's forty-year-old bodies for the first
time. Judging from the shower, from the way she announced it, June's
way would be more casual than wild.

So he would probably have to take off his shirt.

And tell his story again. Well, June, it was like this.... The
story would get in the way, it would snuff the sexy impetus of the
shower. They'd gone out four or five times now. You couldn't delay
these things too long.

All through his ten years married to Christina he'd worn a T-
shirt to bed, most nights anyway—no big deal, it just kept it out of
the way. After a while he could no longer tell if the T-shirt was for him
or for her. It was one of those things you just stop talking about.
Sometimes Christina joked about it, nothing mean, it didn't seem to
bother her. Except that in summer she liked the beach so much, and
of course he didn't. Then it was funny how it worked out, with ozone
and UV starting up and people wearing shirts on the beach just like
him. Suddenly, going to the beach was fine. But by then he and
Christina weren't too fine any more themselves.

The shower stopped. Robert listened to June pad around in her bare feet, bathroom cupboards opening and closing, some kind of plastic container clicking shut. Would she get dressed again? That'd be a little weird. Walk out naked? No. Wrapped in a towel then? They were work friends more than anything, and even though they occupied different floors they bumped into each other once or twice a day, more if they went out of their way to. They had jokey routines that went back years. One of them was going to have to make a leap here. He hoped June came out in the towel.

The Junebug. She was small and cute, and people called her that, or even Bug, and she handled it with grace. If you fight a nickname it has a way of fitting even better. June had a body and a wit that fit the name, but a depth that didn't. She read philosophy and such, names Robert hadn't heard of, and she played bridge tournaments in other cities and won money. They made exactly the same salary, and Robert liked this much more than not.

June came out in a white terrycloth bathrobe. She hadn't wet her hair. With that same smile as before, she held out her hand, made a comic, grunting routine of pulling him up. Led him to the bedroom, no talking, making it easy for them both. They sat on the bed, embraced, kissed. They'd kissed before, and it was comfortable to do now, and easy to take the spirit of the kiss deeper, let the embrace find muscles, and the hands begin their exploring.

Then she was tugging his shirt up, and it was off, and he saw her look. He smiled shyly, shrugged.

"Want to hear about it?"

"About what?" June did a good deadpan.

Robert moved with his family to Lunenburg, Nova Scotia, the summer he turned fifteen, a hard time to move. Friends, Jesus. Harder still that it was from Toronto to a place where everyone talked like farmers and mention of a trip up to Halifax made their eyes bug out. His clothes were all wrong because they were two years ahead, but how do you explain that to guys who are looking at you like you're the most foolish queer they've ever seen? In the fall he'd be entering a school that still had rules about haircuts. Lunenburg was foggy and cold and the weather changed in minutes with no pattern and the feeling was that you couldn't trust the sky at all. It took Robert years to forgive his dad for this, his dad who had moved for no good reason other than a desire to leave a big, heartless city for a small, romantic one.

Robert got into the fringe of a group, one that wasn't too tough or too sucky, mostly jocks, and by midsummer he was playing ball with them, badly, wishing hockey would come soon because he was a bit better at that. It was a shitty feeling, one where people are friendly enough but not really all that interested and it's mostly a sense of you tagging along. They might drop by, see if you wanted to go swimming, or they might not.

Fraser—Frazz—was the leader of the pack. Doug was his best friend. Doug the wild man. The longest hair, curly and kinky so he could get it pretty long before it touched his collar. A glint in his eyes, maybe criminal. There were also Wendell, Ron, Scott. A few others sometimes. Decent guys, but with their own ways, kind of corny. The Maritimes were corny. All of them, even Doug, went to church. But they also drank already. That was maybe the one place they were ahead of Toronto. They drank, and the couple of times they asked Robert along to do this he made an excuse. But then, that one time, he went along. Not that you could in any way blame what happened on booze.

It was the first Saturday in September. School was in two days. This time they did drop by to ask him swimming. It was a half-hour hike to the bend in the river where it was deep enough to dive. They trod the path, sometimes the river rocks, and worked up a sweat. Wendell was sort of Robert's friend now. Wendell was a bit of a goof and not too smart, and Robert could see he was being courted as a best friend because no one else wanted the role. Wendell didn't talk about much except the Boston Bruins and the Boston Red Sox, and he tried to get mock fights going about how crummy "your Leafs" were, but Robert really didn't care about the Leafs one way or the other and couldn't pull it off.

A fly-fisherman in waders was working the pool when they reached it. They considered swimming anyway but recognized him as the uncle of someone they knew. They chose plan B: another pool, shallower, lots of snags, ten minutes upriver. They hiked some more. Doug pulled a mickey of rum out of his jeans, nipped at it, passed it to Frazz and whoever else wanted a taste. Robert didn't, neither did Wendell, but it wasn't a big deal.

At the pool they splashed around a bit to cool off but mostly sat on the rocks. They declared it "some warm" for September, though Robert found it cold. One tree had a decent branch but there was no rope. They moaned about school, and about a girl, Joanie, who was apparently the school beauty but cruelly chaste. Doug and Frazz acted a little drunk, and Wendell sniped at them about "ending up like Gary", who Robert learned was Doug's older brother, who was at present marauding around Halifax drunk or on drugs. Wendell was brave in that he always said what he felt. You had to give him that much.

They were about to leave when Doug, not yet satisfied with the day, or the summer, decided he had to dive from the tree. No amount of warning would sway him, so they stood back, put their faith in his athleticism, watched him take a breath, launch himself in a dive, disappear, and not come up.

They pulled him out fifty feet downriver. His neck was broken and he was dead, no question. Robert was amazed at the next several hours, how deeply hurt his new friends were but how none of them cried; how noble and almost how corny they were as they hiked out, then back in with the paramedics and stretcher; how they insisted on doing all the carrying. And then, after the ambulance pulled away, how they agreed that Frazz's idea was the only one possible. They broke into two groups, stuck out their thumbs, and a few hours later were in Halifax.

It was dark when they drank the rum in the alley behind the tattoo parlour. When the bottle was put into his hand, Robert closed his eyes and gulped and swallowed. It burned and he shuddered, but after that it tasted okay. These guys knew what they were doing. Their good friend dying, a pilgrimage, the rum, this heart-ripe alley. They could do anything tonight and who could possibly blame them? Frazz cried suddenly at one point, as if a glimpse of something crucial had caught him off guard, but then he stood up straighter, smiled grimly, slowly shook his head, had the bottle handed back to him. Robert learned that Frazz and Doug were cousins.

They bought paper and against each other's backs stood and forged letters from their parents, required of minors for tattoos. Frazz had a yearbook picture of Doug, from maybe a few years ago, his baby face, his curly hair. The idea was to have his face and name tattooed over their hearts.

The second bottle of rum was almost gone and they were in a frenzy of promise. Tearful handclasps, heads tilted back to proclaim to the sky, We'll never forget you, man. Never. Scott whirled around and punched a dumpster and broke his hand and no one said a word about it. Jesus. *Doug.* We'll never forget you, man. Robert could see how these guys loved. He wanted to love like them. And be loved like this.

The tattoo parlour was dark and smoky and smelled badly of sweat. The guy was a fat old greaseball with tattoos all over him. He hulked over a huge full ashtray, the pedestal kind that looked stolen from a theatre. He pulled on a beer. Robert found himself not at all afraid. He wished his father would walk in now, not to take him away but to witness this.

The tattoo artist asked for the money first. Frazz and Scott had been in earlier to arrange things, and after hearing Doug's story he'd said, "Dead, eh? Half price." Six guys, six tattoos, sixty bucks. Then they'd gone and found Doug's older brother, Gary, who'd given them all the money they needed but otherwise said nothing and showed not a thing on his face.

They passed the fat man their notes, which from the way he smiled at them you could tell he didn't believe for a second.

"Gets me off the hook," he said, tapping the pile of notes written on identical paper. "So does that." He pointed to a bright red and white sign reading, TATTOOS AT OWN RISK.

"Wash 'er wit' rubbin' alcohol after, you won't have no problems." He paused a second, then said in a loud voice of ritual, "Last chance to walk away." He looked at each of them in turn, eyes dead, not really caring, the money pressed flat in his tight shirt pocket.

"So who first?"

Robert didn't hesitate. He was stepping forward, taking off his shirt, getting in the chair, a long deep breath. He heard Wendell's, "You don't even have to, man," but ignored him. The fat guy chuckled, lit a smoke, opened a beer, said it kept him steady, chuckled again.

The guy pressed the photo to Robert's breastbone with one hand and worked the needle-gun with the other. The pain was good hard pain but it was easy. Over the chirr of the needle Robert heard whispers through clenched teeth: Won't forget you, Doug-man. No way, Doug-man.

Before too long Robert was spun in the chair to face the others and the tattoo artist said, "That's the face." No one said anything, and the artist added, "Looks way better after a few days, eh? What's the name again?" Robert was spun back. Doug, someone said.

The artist chuckled again. He asked, "So how ya spell Doug then?"

"D-U-G," someone said in an extra-dumb voice, adding to the artist's joke, no one in the room hearing the sad embarrassment in the artist's question.

And then later when Robert was spun at them again, they looked, their breath caught, and someone yelled, "Jesus Christ you stupid fat asshole!" More yelling, some money thrown in their faces, a few punches. Then they were outside to rage and laugh in the alleys of Halifax until the dawn came and they could put their thumbs out and hope they made Lunenburg in time for tomorrow and school.

Robert's father never did steal enough law practice from the other lawyer in town, who happened to have been born there, and the family returned to Toronto a year after they'd come. Robert took back with him the tattoo of a misspelled name and what looked like a child's hasty line-drawing of a girl's face.

It was maybe a week after he'd gotten the tattoo that Robert realized he and Doug had never once talked to each other.

She had slipped the robe back on as he talked. He kept his chest bared. She traced it now with a finger, a Junebug sort of gesture. But what she said was too ironic to be cute: "Too bad you're not sixteen. The punk enigma thing. You'd be, like, really really totally cool."

That was the story. There was nothing more to say. Sex felt distant now. It would be his turn to make a leap, and even that might not get them back to it.

"So." He reached up to stroke her cheek. He tried a coy smile himself. "What now?"

"Did you hitch home and show your parents?"

"No."

"When did they find out?"

"They never did."

"Ah."

Her look told him he wasn't finished talking.

"They were worried about my addiction to T-shirts."

But his joking wasn't enough. June was meditative.

"You've hated it all your life."

The word "hate" was maybe a little too simple, but he shrugged and nodded.

"Why didn't you go get it taken off? Removed?"

June watched while he considered his answer. Before he could speak she touched his arm, said, "Wait a sec," and left the room. She popped her head back in to tell him, "That looks pretty dangerous on a bureaucrat. I think it turns me on something fierce," and then just as quickly left. He decided he loved her for saying that. Maybe he loved her altogether. He could see living with her, the ease of it, the good far outweighing the bad.

He heard her opening and pouring wine. He wasn't at all clear about what he'd be telling her next. Why hadn't he just removed it? She'd left out another possibility—it was no problem at all to cover a tattoo with a darker, better one. He had pictured an eagle, a snake. The logo of the Leafs. Or the funny-logical one he'd considered longest: a heart. A heart where his heart was.

Back in Toronto, only his doctor knew, a doctor Robert pledged to secrecy before he would take his shirt off. Through him Robert got a note excusing him from showers after gym—a skin condition.

Robert was aware of his perverse yearning even while it was growing. He began to hold dear the memory of his buddies back in Nova Scotia. He and Wendell wrote letters for two or three years, and Robert got good enough at liking the Leafs to trade insults about Boston. Wendell referred to "the tattoo night" once, but Robert didn't refer to it back.

He knew his nostalgia was curious. Nostalgia for a year of loneliness and embarrassment. He'd catch himself in false memories that he really had become their friend. That he'd been with them on that midnight search for survivors of the swamped trawler, that he'd been to their kitchen parties, that he'd been told their secrets.

Perhaps odder still, he shied away from all friends now, especially the back-slapping jock kind, and parties, especially parties with alcohol. He knew a bottle of beer was not going to land him in a tattoo parlour—he could even laugh at this notion—but at the same time he kept away.

Girls too. Girls were hard. He went on dates, but with every jerky step taken in the direction of sexiness, no minute passed without him worrying how it would be when the shirt came off.

The first time he told a girl, he learned that telling would never become an easy thing. The event resulted from a night's wrestling on a blanket in the back yard, his parents away. Sheila, ostensibly on a sleep-over at a girlfriend's, for some reason wouldn't go into the house with him, as if being in the house was an extra lubricant to sin. Still, on the blanket in the yard they did everything but the final sin, and after, trying for something like love, Robert told her. Her questions were tentative. Worse, they gave rise to an old, visceral sourness he hadn't tasted much of late.

"So were all the other ones spelled wrong too?"

"No. No, they weren't."

One question in particular got the sourness up, and his face swelled with it.

"You must've really loved the guy? Doug?"

He nodded. "I guess so."

So he told her but didn't tell her. And understood now that telling a person also meant telling himself.

It got to be that his tattoo became his gauge of a girl. Robert would consider someone and say to himself, "I could tell her." Or even, "I want to tell her." Though this was rare. Rarest of all was him saying to himself, "I could wear her face on my chest."

Graduating from high school, moving forward with his eyes set on the unremarkable—a commerce degree—Robert avoided friends and all women save those he wanted to tell. He began to use his tattoo as a measure, a litmus test, for all merit. What, he took to asking himself—what car, what food, what professor's idea, what philosophy of right—could be worn, for ever, with love, on his chest? When he caught himself at the test he knew it was silly, but all the same he discovered in time that hardly anything in life met the standard.

"Maybe if—" June laughed, interrupting herself. They were into the second bottle of wine. "Maybe if we both tattoo *MacLean* on ourselves he won't be mad when we come in all late and hung over tomorrow." Grant MacLean was their boss, new at the job and top-heavy in arrogance and paranoia.

"Or 'Grant is God'."

"Grant is good, Grant is good, Grant is good."

Work tomorrow would be a write-off, but a pain they would share.

They laughed about bad tattoos that might have been. What if you had to endure today the stuff you thought was so great when you were young—Bilbo Baggins, Paul McCartney, a Mustang convertible? June ran down the rest of her list in her head, her smile falling at the end of it.

"What?" Robert asked.

"I'm really glad I don't have a tattoo of this guy named Luke on me."

"How long were you and Luke—"

"Maybe a few months. I would've tattooed his name on my forehead if he'd wanted me to."

Robert finished his glass of wine. At this, June sank back onto the bed. On an elbow, he leaned over her, then bent to kiss her. It might happen now.

"You're lucky," she whispered, swirling a finger on Doug. "You didn't know the guy long enough to hate him."

"That's maybe," he opened her robe, "that's maybe the most cynical thing about people I've ever heard."

"Yeah," she said. "Maybe." Was she warning him about herself? Was she warning herself about him? She looked sincere when she told him, "But this, I like it on you. I love it on you."

"I'm glad."

"Thanks for telling me."

"You're welcome."

"It keeps everything young."

Not quite knowing what she meant by that, and not quite knowing what he was doing now, he raised himself over her, climbing forward on the bed so that his chest was over her face. He lowered himself and kissed her with Doug. She kissed Doug back, seriously, not smiling. Robert had a funny thought then, rising out of the deeper thought that maybe he did love this woman. The funny thought was how easy it would be to have a tattoo artist draw a horizontal line through the D. Which would make it a B, which would make the name BUG, which would make the face hers.

WISDOM

JANICE SIPPED COFFEE AT THE OLD DINING-ROOM TABLE, the sun too hot on her back. She remembered how, as a teenager, her letter-day had always been a time of portent. She remembered waking up in this house ready for rainbows, or thunder, or heavenly weeping. Now she found she anticipated tomorrow with something more like weariness. The thought occurred that maybe her weariness reflected her father's own as he wrote the last ones. The letters had grown tired. Careless. Already kind of dead. That was the word, why not use it?

Was it so weird that his state of being while writing might affect her directly? Though here she was in portent land again. Not the rainbows or thunder, but weeping—weeping, no problem. Dad still could make her cry. And that was fine, that was fine. Of course it was.

Tomorrow Janice would turn thirty-three and she would read his last letter to her, his last to any of them.

She switched chairs. Her black T-shirt was why the sun was so hot. Why had she worn it? Mom might feel it as disrespectful or something. She'd always taken their fashions personally, especially the punky stuff. A black T didn't go with the occasion, didn't go with this corny smash of flowers—a couple of dozen daisies—Mom had cut and filled the blue vase with to centre the table. That old vase. Janice could remember being warned away from it as a toddler.

She listened to the familiar sounds of her mother clinking away at the sink. Forty years in that small kitchen. Mom could pretty much stand in the middle and reach anything, eyes closed, pivoting, grabbing, arms smart as typists' fingers.

Singing now as she worked. Singing because two of her children were coming to have dinner and spend the night, and because the third, Richard the Wayward, Dick the Prick, had said he'd bless them with a call in the morning, after the letter. Janice had not often heard her shy mom sing so brazenly. You could almost hear a melody. No matter how old kids got, apparently to a mother there was nothing perverse about having them sleep over. "You kids," Mom still said. Ivy, thirty-nine, and huge, had two grown kids of her own. Janice, divorced, trying out a partnership with Ron—who because of her use of that word called her "pardner", and who this morning had given her an assessing look as she left with her overnight bag for Mom's. Tomorrow she'd be thirty-three, wild in itself. And Richard was thirty now. Richard had survived another milestone. Richard the Always Alone. Janice saw him as a sneering fox in the night, and still a child for this.

Mom's children were bloated, worn, damaged adults. Mom singing over the hum of the microwave. If not just two but all three of them—imagine—if all three had agreed to sleep over tonight, crammed in the old bedroom, jammies on, whining for hot chocolate, Mom would be in there belting out opera.

Families were sad machines by definition, weren't they? Kids flew the coop, feuds, death, whatever, it was just a sad matter of time. Breakup built right in. Automatic. Guaranteed.

Janice snorted a laugh. Little Richard, overweight and chain-smoking and scowling, bulging in his Expos jammies while Mom yo-delled in with hot chocolate.

Then it occurred to her that her mother's song—that her mother might be in there singing because tomorrow it would all be over. Tomorrow, the last time Mom would have to hand over one of his letters.

As a young girl coming to understand what her father did for a living, she held a generally sad image of him behind the counter at the post office. She was worried for him that all that mail he received from people's hands—the love letters, the birthday cards (some with money) and thank-you notes, the funny letters from best friends, the thin blue letters from foreign lands—all that great mail was lick-closed and secret in envelopes and he never got to read a word. None. Never.

"Well I can't, Jannie," he explained once, smiling as if her question was the only thing strange about this.

Later came a different sadness, one tinged with the disgust of a teenager watching a parent plunge into fallibility. Visiting him at the post office, taking him lunch or whatever, she learned about the menial nature of the work, the fingering through people's change on the counter. She'd walk in and see him there in his blue shirt, tired-on-his-feet, serving someone, then staring off while the next customer approached, and she'd realize that in these ten seconds she was seeing not only his entire day but his entire life.

She leaned in and smelled a daisy. It smelled half flower, half weed. Childhood. She remembered his saying, "You have to stop and smell the flowers." Or maybe that had been in a letter. His life and his letters were so mixed together now. But he never seemed to know that clichés were clichés.

He was a sucker for the corny. She remembered him coming back once from the doctor, whistling. He'd been told his ribcage pain was just him getting older, cartilage shrinking, no room for the ribs. He was "settling like a good old wooden house". Dad liked this corny image so much he didn't mind his pain for a while. The power of doctors, amazing. With an arrogant mistake and corny phrase they could temporarily heal a man with cancer in the lungs, the brain, the bones, and make him whistle.

When she was home for letter-days it was especially easy to remember, to picture. The last weeks before he left for the hospital. The thinning ginger hair. (Only Richard had inherited their father's hair, thank God.) His pale skin getting almost see-through, even the freckles disappearing. His enfeebled walk through this dining-room on his way to see Mom in the kitchen—the walk getting slower and slower, then that ugly shuffling, then the rented wheelchair, and then, simply, bed, him exhausted on the bed. As she delivered glasses of juice or whatever, she sensed from the way he was lying there that he wasn't so much sick and dying as exhausted.

Age forty-two. Seemed old then.

He died when she was nine. Tomorrow's letter would be his twenty-fourth to her. Time flies. She could remember him saying that, too. *Boy*, does time fly—he said it like that.

The very first letter had moved her, maybe dented her, more than any other. Of course her first experience of opening a letter from Dad, who was dead, was going to be weird no matter what. Plus, it was a surprise. She was ten that day. They'd just finished cake. An envelope was clean and cold in her hand, Mom saying, maybe you want to read it in private. Then she was alone in the bedroom the three of them shared. The others out there waiting. She stood just inside the closed door, breathing hard, almost sobbing already. A surprise. Mom had brought this box out and tipped it at them to show all these letters. She said they'd get one every birthday. The hurt, since Dad, had gotten less like everyone had said it would, but standing here with this letter made it come back big as ever. She opened it. There were his words, and the blue ink of his post office pen.

That first one had also been the shortest. It had said, "What makes me most sad of all is not seeing you grow up, Janice. But who knows, maybe I will. Love, Dad."

Maybe this initial brevity was just Dad getting going, because the letters would get longer. Or maybe he did mean this one most of all, and there was really nothing more to say. Whatever the case, the words sank in deep and, for years, for years and years, Janice caught herself wondering at the happiest of times and at the saddest of times if the feeling she felt was Dad watching her grow up. When she passed her last swimming badge, was that Dad above her in the pool, watching? When she stole the Aero bar at the corner, was that Dad? Was that Dad when Marky Christianson unhooked her bra? Sometimes she felt him as clear as could be, so much so that she tried to talk to him. Other times he was nowhere and never had been. It took years for the feeling to leave, to leave the room, to leave the sky. Whatever that feeling was—she would acquire words to try out on it: guilt, self-consciousness, superego—whatever that feeling was, for years it kept her from doing all kinds of things.

He had work-wit, little jokes for customers. People seemed to like them, but they made Janice blush. Counting back change—say a dollar bill, then three cents—he'd go, "Here's a hundred pennies. And three, great, big ones." For a joke he'd talk louder and not smile, and he'd look off to the side, a kind of over-the-counter cool. But Janice could see his head quivering with something electric inside. Sliding fourteen cents across the counter, he'd go, "Fourteen, hundred, dollars. Be careful with it." Or when he took a thin envelope from a child, or even an adult sometimes, he might put it next to his ear and shake it and ask, "Any monkeys in there?" Never smiling. Then he'd turn away with their envelope and flick it into one of three bins.

It was Richard who, after watching the *Revenge of the Nerds* movie, said, "Dad's an adult nerd." They made him promise never to call Dad a nerd to his face. Though Dad might've risen to it, nerdlike. He might've said, "I am so!" That was one he did at home. If Mom accused him of being too shy with the waiter or whoever, he'd say. "I am so!" Saying it, his head would quiver.

One of his little work jokes Janice almost liked. Asking a co-worker if Ed, say, was on coffee break, he'd go, "Ed gone to Florida yet?" Or announcing the start of his own break he'd go, "Well, I'm off to Florida."

Ivy clomped in, mid-afternoon. She had a suitcase with her, a big one on wheels, and her chiropractic pillow under an arm. Equipped for comfort, she liked to say. Ready to relax. She had their father's corny way, but was better at it. Ivy shouted from the hall, "Hey Mom, hey Jan," and went straight to the bedroom.

Ivy's last letter, the last she'd ever get, had gone on about the fact that it was her birthday, and that she was now almost as old as he was. He'd ended it with, "So, happy birthday? Are you happy you were born? I hope so." Sometimes you could see him reaching, you could see him trying to give lessons, make them think. Which was good, it was good. Janice herself liked those letters best, because even if they were obvious—minor spiritual pep talks—they showed her what Dad considered important.

Ivy didn't come out for twenty minutes. Then Janice heard her cross the hall in her slippers and start taking a shower. Ivy called these visits "vacations from the kids", but Janice knew her sister had been in their old bedroom, sitting there on the bed, looking intently around.

Why, after more than twenty letters, was she expecting something from him? Why was she still hoping for life's secrets, for pith? Janice knew her fading hope was that a reservoir of wisdom lay behind his shyness, and that in these letters he would reveal it.

As if. One letter, in her teens, read: "When you start going on dates, don't do anything I wouldn't do. Ha ha. I don't want to be a grandfather yet. Ha ha again. Here's a joke I heard about birth control pills—the best birth control pill is an aspirin held firmly between the knees. Remember that teenage boys are dogs. Some are nice dogs, but they are dogs even though they will pretend they aren't. When they wait for you at the front door and no one can see them their eyes look just like dogs eyes."

So, what—Janice watched herself gulp her coffee, felt rising anger that was probably just like Richard's—what had she been supposed to feel about stuff like that? Had that been *Dad,* or Dad with his brain half gone?

One thing she did learn from him in those last months. He taught her what death was. He taught her that death begins when you're still alive. And that it kills every part of you, your body, and your heart, and your mind. He taught her that dying steals all you have that is good, and that this process is mean, and ugly, and nothing but shitty. He taught her this though he hadn't meant to. He was just the tool. Sitting in his wheelchair, staring off, losing more body and more brain and more will, he was what teachers call a visual aid.

At one point they agreed that Mom was writing them. They thought that maybe she saw it as a way to keep his influence alive or something, a way to give them a two-parent family. And, it was a damn smart way for her to fix problems as they came up. The coincidence of some letters they got in their troublesome teens, for instance. Dad's timely advice, right. Brilliant ploy, Mom. But it was so clever, they decided in the end, that it couldn't be her. No way. It was Dad, and that one letter to Richard was an accident, just a weird coincidence.

It wasn't just that particular letter that did it. Richard had always been sensitive. At age six, right after his dad died, he built, with walls of cardboard and scrap, a bedroom for himself in the basement. Well, Ivy being fifteen, the time was certainly ripe. Their mother got some bamboo curtains and a carpet for the cement, and built a proper job out of Richard's pathetic beginning, but nobody liked the idea of a six-year-old in the basement by himself, and so soon after losing his father.

Richard grew a visible edge, one that sharpened instead of weathered in the tumble of life's obstacles. Their mother called his a "strong" personality. Not many people liked him. Mom more than once explained to the sisters that, well, no wonder it was hardest on him. He was the youngest, and the son, and he and Dad had been closest, probably, or at least—Mom's voice softening—your father wanted them to be closest, no offence. But, girls, it was obvious from the letter.

Janice thought, still thought, that that letter had scared Richard more than anything. She remembered him standing there, sixteen that morning, wearing the leather-like black jacket from Mom, holding the letter Mom had just handed him. Richard looked up from the envelope and sneered. "I hate this," he said. It was clear he'd always wanted to say it. "I hate it." Mom whispered, "Aw, Richie." But Richard looked at her and explained something. "He's selfish. He just wanted to always hog in and make everybody still feel bad. He's *selfish.*"

Then he ripped open the letter right in front of them, punishing them with this casualness. He held it up, rattling it, telling them with his glare and shrug that this thing was a fortune cookie and that's all. He started to read—"I love you much more..."—then his eyes hit a word and stuck there. He dropped the letter and turned and left, and he didn't come home, Mom said, till sometime near dawn.

What the letter said was, "I love you much more than anything or anyone. When I think of how much I love you, I realize it is the only time I am not being selfish."

It was just one of those things you couldn't explain. Other letters had come close to feeling as if they were charmed, connected, but they were just a case of Dad guessing and getting it right. Anticipating. It was a pretty safe bet that you could write to a fifteen-year-old about unrequited love and she'd have something like that going on in her life right then.

That was a strange one though, Richard's sixteenth. Janice had, for a while, looked for portents again. Ivy it seemed to have made aggressively bored—when her day came she pretended not to care. But the amount of time she spent in the bedroom with her letter, and the amount of silence coming hard off her all day, spoke of something that was not boredom at all.

King Richard stopped sharing his letters with any of them. Then, a decade ago, he'd taken Janice to their old bedroom and, with an evil smile, brought a shoebox down from the upper closet shelf beyond Mom's reach. In it, a bunch of unopened envelopes. On them was written "Richard 17", "Richard 18", "Richard 19", in Dad's hand. Janice stared at them. They took a second to register. They looked overripe. They were old bones holding living marrow. There were secrets alive in there. Involuntarily her hands went to them, but Richard said, Fuck no, and shoved them back up on the shelf, out of sight.

Mom sliced the roast at the table. Ivy—whom Janice couldn't help but see as a huge pudgy girl herself—talked about her daughter Beth. Beth was very frank, and Ivy had picked up the habit, and was repeating a conversation they'd had about Beth's boyfriend's refusal to wear condoms.

"Jerrod said that absolutely no men like them, they feel awful," Ivy said, pouring gravy on her potatoes. "I dunno.... Makes me wanna take one loonnng coffee break."

"I don't like the boy," their mother said simply, holding up the bowl of peas for Janice, waiting for her to finish dishing herself some potatoes.

"Just put them down, Mom," Janice told her, indicating with her chin the large open table space. Her mother waited with the peas aloft.

Dinner was sad, though this wasn't voiced. Richard had been partly right. Selfishness wasn't the word, but the letters had kept Dad alive in a way. After tomorrow, he'd only be dead.

So complex were her feelings around this, Janice didn't know what to think. She felt relief, she felt panic. Something else in her was ready to weep like a girl, weep for days. She had tried to explain to Ron her week's silence, but she hadn't found words.

Nor could she tell what her mother felt, but then she never could. Mom, who'd not been left a single letter of her own, had conducted each letter-day with what looked like simple loving concern, an unquestioning custodian of her husband's last wish. But Janice had a sense that she might be tired of the whole scenario. And the letter-days had grown ragged of late. Dad had somehow missed Richard's twenty-eighth—no letter at all—and it was one of the rare birthdays he'd come to. Then Ivy's letters had run out a year too early. Janice would be getting two letters after Ivy's last. Well, they'd all seen Dad's failing ways, no explanations necessary. But who could say what Richard had felt on his twenty-eighth birthday? Who could say what Ivy was feeling now?

Odd, the reactions to the letters. Dad couldn't have known. For instance, over the years his letters to Ivy had grown more and more mischievous, and this seemed to Janice to have had the effect of making Ivy more serious. Again, Dad and Ivy had the same humour—sometimes Janice was startled hearing Ivy joke. But Ivy would emerge in tears from the bedroom with a letter that said only, "You get what you get only if you get it?" She'd avoid Janice's eyes, shaking her head, her letter-day ruined, her anticipation slapped in the face by foolishness.

Sounds of his entrance hidden by the clatter of dishes being cleared, there stood Richard, looking blankly at them, surprise, surprise. He accepted dessert, and their mother's grateful hellos, expert at being prodigally bored. He shrugged at the question of his staying the night, took his slice of pie to the couch and flicked on the TV.

"I *love* your hair," Mom called from the safety of the kitchen. Richard's hair was black. *Black*-black, one of those punk shades that trumpets the fact that it's dye. A couple of years ago he'd shown up with his hair yellow as opposed to blond. This hair looked extra black and ugly-on-purpose against his translucent skin. A redhead's skin. Dad's.

"I *love* it," Mom called again, as if to a girlfriend, emerging from the kitchen in a waft of fresh coffee smell. She'd been beaming since his arrival. Janice wondered if Mom thought her son gay. Janice didn't think so herself.

"Not the point, Mom," Richard told her, and he slid Janice, fellow-punk in her black T-shirt, a wink.

Sometimes Richard just turned her stomach. Nothing complex in the feeling at all.

They settled into the TV sitcoms. Mom got up and down several times until nobody wanted anything else. Janice knew how much Mom wanted to talk, nothing specific, just to hear about their lives. But she sat and faced the TV, watching them as much as it, happy enough.

Richard dozed, then sat up for Seinfeld. Mom perked up too, for now her kids were laughing out loud a little, not together, just here and there. Janice saw her mom trying to like it, smiling when one of them laughed.

In the end you never knew what to think, that was the problem. Even after tearing into the letters and analysing like crazy. Richard had a point when he said, "You suck on words that long, you'll find exactly what you want."

There was always something to debate. Janice remembered an early one to Ivy that said, "I know one day you'll all have jobs and your own places but when I picture you in the future you're always together playing cards at the dining-room table, one chair empty. Or maybe not."

Sometimes he got maudlin like that, the empty chair part, which was fine. At least you could understand it. But what about the "or maybe not"? The possibilities were clear. One, the noble option, meant their mother remarrying—his chair would not stay empty. Two, the whiny option, implied that they might just remove his chair. Three, the spooky option, suggested the chair wouldn't be empty at all—he'd be sitting there watching them. And then four, the cynical option, referred not to the chair but to the family and reassessed the whole scenario: the family might not get together much.

Well, they didn't often get together at the dining-room table for cards. But they did gather there on letter-days, passing around the latest letter. There was often an empty chair, unless Richard had come by to sit in it.

Janice woke up first. A beautiful morning, she took a walk through her old neighbourhood on that stretch where he'd taught her to ride her new bike, it was pink, with rainbow tassels. She'd climbed to the top of that old tree, and Richard had cried until she came down. And there she'd been in the back seat with Marky Christianson when Mom walked by and pretended she didn't know Mark's car.

As on other letter-days, she tried to conjure Dad, but he just wasn't in many memories. The bike lesson even—it was as if she remembered the memory, not the reality. She did remember him behind the counter at work, she remembered him at the lake that time falling-out-of-the-boat-on-purpose, she thought she remembered the smell of the skin of his neck, and some playful words in her ear—but otherwise, visually, he just hadn't sunk in much.

Walking, Janice tried to picture him alone in the morning, his wheelchair rolled up to the desk while the rest of them still slept. He wrote all the letters there, over the course of three days. The window facing the desk showed him the maple tree and the hedge. He pauses in thought—what to write next? what will help my children? what will make them laugh, or think?—and then he lifts his head at the sound of a bird, a chickadee, its call the sound of the sunrise itself. He is alive.

Richard was up when she got back. Sitting on the couch in his peach underwear, stretching, the blankets on the floor. He looked too old for his underwear and his hair. Bags under his eyes. Not looking at her, he yawned and said, "Today's the day."

So he'd been paying attention.

"I guess it is."

Janice made coffee in the kitchen. Richard joined her and lurked beside the dripping maker. He'd pulled on his pants but his upper body was bare. She felt strange seeing it—skinny, a bruise on the ribs she knew he wouldn't tell her about even if she asked—still it was her little brother's upper body.

"I didn't get you anything," Richard said, peering into the fridge.

"I'll make you breakfast."

"Yeah, right."

"No, I will. Pancakes." He pulled a small plastic tub from the freezer and shook it at her. "Boo-blerry."

Janice was suddenly hugging him from behind. She held on hard for a few seconds before he wriggled away. Blueberry pancakes, their father's favourite, pronounced this way after one of their early attempts at the word.

Richard had his skinny back to her, making breakfast. He moved expertly. Well, why not—he was a bachelor, he cooked for himself. Maybe he made himself boo-blerry pancakes.

It was just—she had to leave the kitchen for fear of crying—it was just that he had never said such a corny, defenceless thing in his life.

Nobody had a present for Janice. At breakfast Ivy and her mother whispered about this, amazed at having both forgotten. They laughed confessing it to her, and made elaborate promises of gifts and lunches out. Poor Janice, her mother kept saying. But no one really cared, least of all Janice. Their having forgotten gifts was nothing in the face of this day.

After breakfast, Janice stopped her mother from starting on the dishes.

"Let's just do it, Mom."

Her mother wouldn't look at her. She wiped her clean hands on the dishtowel, and wiped them again. "Okay," she whispered, and walked off quickly.

She returned with the box, walking more slowly. She set it down gently on the coffee table.

She removed the last envelope—on which was printed, "Janice 33"—but her gaze lingered on the box, empty now.

Her hands went to her face. "Oh dear...his damn box. What am I going to do with this?"

Ivy got to her crying mother first, and held her. Janice looked at the old box. It was the original box, a thin kind of cardboard you didn't see any more. It had discoloured to brown and was held together by crisscrosses of yellowed tape, some of which crumbled at the touch. She saw now that this was her mother's letter, always had been. It was the envelope that held all the others, and her mother got to open it three times a year.

Janice examined the envelope in her hand. She didn't want to wait. It felt right to share it, to read it with them, and it felt right to read it while her mother was crying. Then they could mourn together.

"I'll read it to you, Mom," Janice whispered, and her mother nodded rapidly through her tears.

Janice got her thumb under a loose edge and lifted, ripping the brittle paper. The page inside was still perfectly white. She eased it out. It was folded like all the others, into three.

The morning sun flooded in bright on the daisies, and on them all, emboldening. Richard squinted at her in the light, his body crinked awkwardly in the chair. Ivy, looking simple and big-eyed, kept an arm around their mother's shoulder.

Janice unfolded the letter, and appeared to read. Her quick laughter startled them. Her mother lifted her head. Ivy's eyes got bigger. Richard said *What*.

"It's—"

Janice laughed again, but there were tears now too, and she felt her face contorting, though she felt fine, she felt fine.

"It's—him."

She laughed and waved the bright page at her family. It was blank. They didn't laugh yet, so she said, "Look!" and held it up closer to them, white and clean and perfect, this picture of his spirit, free now at last, this portrait he'd drawn of himself, whether he'd meant to or not.

ANGELS KILL HUMMINGBIRDS

IT WAS SUNDAY NOON IN HIS NEW APARTMENT, a fine autumn day, no
wind for once, so Alan took his coffee out to the balcony, four storeys
up, nice. Then the phone. All his cousin Jon said was, Heart attack,
it's Dad, he's here at the house. Then hung up.

Alan paused, as usual after a call from his relatives. There
were obvious questions. If Uncle Ross had just had a heart attack,
what was he doing at home? And Jon hated his father—had he been
brief because of emergency, or had it all been more like a shrug? There
was another question: he could have sworn he'd heard Aunt Alice in
the background, and it had sounded as if she was singing.

He hadn't been across the river in months. He'd had enough
of being mocked for going back to school in his thirties. That scorn
for anything not theirs. Starting his car he felt the twisty stomach that
always came with a visit. He knew he'd end up raking their leaves or
something again, then felt guilty thinking this. But nothing over there
was ever simple, it always verged on a nonsense fight, a web of things
not said, and everyone was to blame, even him.

Going over the bridge, he saw he was driving too fast. Maybe
it was in fact an emergency and they didn't know what to do. Squeal-
ing round the off-ramp he passed a cop who either didn't notice or
care. He could hear himself explain: "My uncle's had a heart attack.
Maybe. Probably not."

He crunched the gravel of their long drive shaped like a broken bone for no reason at all, no trees to cause the jagged little turn.
To the left the shitheap of rusted vehicles was almost covered, finally,
with brush. A car approached and he passed, on her way out (and not

looking concerned), what was probably another of Jon's girlfriends. Dyed blonde, apparently Jon's only trigger for lust.

His cousin was forty, paunchy, jobless for life. If Jon forgot himself and laughed he showed pulled-tooth spaces. If he went shirtless there was that tomato tattoo. He'd had long hair as far back as Alan had memories, and lived on his parents' acre in a home-made two-roomer he called The Loft. Impossibly, women still came around. Somewhere along the line Jon had decided to make a mystery of himself—to simple questions he would stare deeply off and say nothing—but Alan figured the only thing mysterious about Jon was how he'd learned that trick at all. There wasn't a deep thinker in the family, including himself, Alan could confess this. His cousin Daphne—Jesus: dyed-blonde Daphne, Jon's girlfriends. Who knows what family really does to people? Cousin Daphne, gone twenty years now, had been smart enough to leave as soon as it was legal.

Well, there was Aunt Alice. But Alice was not so much deep as sideways. He would not forgive her mocking his quest for the forestry degree, happy with herself: "Who needs books for trees? When they're ripe, pick 'em!" And that one time, the stinger, "Don't matter to anybody how big ya get, Bonny-boy."

He parked outside the disorder of their four cars but pointed his for an exit home, or to the hospital.

Rapping on the door, he went in. Alice was alone downstairs. She didn't look up from her magazine. Alan scanned for a glass or bottle, but couldn't see one, and she looked steady. She sat unmoving in her rocker, humming a jazzy something, wearing a bright green sweater. The magazine was *Musician*. On its cover was a black horn player, beaded dreadlocks, half her age. Alice's hair was teased out big, a style she called "early Grace Slick". Since Alice had quit the stage her hair was the one thing she'd kept up. Decades now. Alan had seen the pictures a million times, the black and white glossies she used to leave lying around. According to Jon they were from a jazz club one summer in Montreal, the time she'd made inroads there.

"Hi Alice."

"Hi there Al, Bonny-boy."

"What's this with Uncle Ross?"

"Who called you?"

"Did he have a heart attack?"

"He's upstairs."

"Is he all right?"

"Since when's he been all right?" Head still in her magazine, but happy with her joke.

"Jon said he had a heart attack?"

"I think he was all right once in kindergarten, one day at lunch, mouth full of somethin', big stupid eyes...." Alice did a puffy, bug-eyed face. "Still eats like that. His idea of sex, too."

"Upstairs?"

"Ask him yourself. How would I know with that man." Flipping a page of her magazine, she pretended to read it.

He climbed the stairs, not looking forward to this. When he reached the landing and stood regarding his uncle's door, from below Aunt Alice began wailing softly, an ambulance siren shaped through a sly smile. Alan recognized this as the singing he'd heard over the phone.

He knocked, waited, didn't hear anything. He knocked again, opened the door, peered in. Uncle Rossy was lying rigidly on his bed, head propped up with two pillows, glaring at him already. That stiff hair, which always reminded Alan of anger.

"Hi Uncle Ross."

The old man said, like a challenge, "I might die."

It was Aunt Alice who years ago had suggested Alzheimer's, though it hadn't meant much. She called her husband many things. But he was confused and mean, and he'd been progressing this way for years. Even at night when Alice had been long into the wine, Ross was the stupider of the two. Their meanness to each other was maybe equal, though hers seemed less because she was sometimes funny with it.

"What you think's wrong?"

"Jesus boy, I don't think—I *know*. How many times!" He huffed like a petulant girl, eyes skyward in frustration.

His posture was strange, prone but so erect, so stiff he was almost convex on the bed, maybe a pain wouldn't let him relax. He was too red as well. Every third or fourth breath he had to dig down for.

"Jon called me. Have—"

"Fuck does he know."

"He said heart attack."

"He did, did he?" Uncle Ross sneered, mocking Jon and Alan both, then turned away with a dismissive shake of the head, leaving

Alan, as usual, not knowing what had just been said.

"Do you want to go to the hospital?"

"That what *she* told you?"

"No, do *you* think *you* should go to the hospital."

"Oh!" Ross did a hoarse, ugly attempt at being effeminate. "You care."

Awful old bastard. That was what the university thing meant to him—Alan was now an intellectual, uppity, and therefore homosexual. Jesus, unbelievable, why be bothered.

"I am asking you if you are sick."

"Ahh, it all hurts." Ross turned his head to the wall. He crossed his big old mechanic's hands on his chest. Breathing came harder for him. "Leave me, the hell, alone. Tell her, to get me some, water."

Maybe this was just a big baby thing. Maybe they'd had a fight and he'd resorted to being pathetic. He didn't generally go that route.

Downstairs, neither of them speaking, Alan passed Alice. The twist in his stomach was deep now, ripe. Why did he ever come here? He filled a glass at the sink.

"What's he doing?" Alice asked from her magazine.

So there was some concern. "He's laying down. He looks sort of red. Says he hurts all over."

"Maybe it's his heart."

"And we're sitting here! Jesus Alice!"

"Well hey, we gotta go sometime, Bonny-boy." A little smile. "What're you pouring there?"

"Water." Okay, why not try. "He wants you to take this up to him. I gotta go talk to Jon."

Alice nodded without looking up. "He's out by the stream. He wants you to help get his boat out."

It couldn't be, it just couldn't be the reason Jon had phoned. To get his boat out. Though Jon had done similar. He'd phone up and chide him for ignoring his lonely old aunt and uncle, a rehearsed, "You're all they have, Al-man. And they're all you have too." But as soon as he got there Jon would have some two-man chore that needed doing and before Alan could so much as say hi to his lonely old aunt and uncle he'd be hefting this into the rafters or dragging that out of the rot-stink ditch.

Jon was at the river's edge, fishing with a rod that was missing the top eyelet. He was pulling something in, and while the bottom two-thirds of the rod was arced, the top third stuck out straight and useless, ugly. At his feet, half filled with water and leaves, his old wooden rowboat lay waiting for two men to dump it then haul its waterlogged sadness across to the shed.

Jon brought in a chub, lifting it out by the line. Sometimes it still felt good to see him, like a brother he'd never had. That one year they'd made a point to play chess, and played often—beer chess, they'd called it. But the less Alan came over the river the less connected to his cousin he felt. He'd been visiting less and less for years, ever since Uncle Ross lost his job and was always home. Who wanted to come here with a man like that around?

He watched his cousin squeeze the fish at the throat, pulling this way and that, trying to free a deep hook. Alan could hear its gills ripping. No, it wasn't just Ross. It was the family.

He recalled the time, telling this English major he was hot on (and trying a sort of rags-to-riches angle) that his family was white trash. But she only got mad, claiming that the expression was the most racist imaginable, that the word "white" assumed that real trash, expected trash, was black. He apologized by making a joke of it, saying, "I'm just plain trash then," but that looked to be it for them and it was mutual. Watching her, just her mouth smiling, her eyes were foreign to him, and he saw himself then as no different from his cousin, comfortable with the women at Rockin' Rodeo, women who laughed easily to quips about hooters.

His cousin dropped the chub onto the rocks of the bank, an inch or two from the water, where it flapped, ignored. Jon studied his fingers, all the time in the world, then wiped the blood and bits of gill onto his shirt. He looked up and smiled at Alan, showing his gap teeth, helping the dying fish into the water with his foot as he did so.

They passed the bowl of mashed potatoes around like a normal family, though they had to serve themselves with their own forks. Sundays his relatives did often sit down like this, to an actual meal. Otherwise it was a sandwich here, fried meat there, sometimes just the one thing. Alan remembered meals of a pack of bacon, or crackers and cheese, or even a bag of cookies. Jon had for the last dozen years taken over Ross's old job of growing tomatoes against the sunny wall of the house, and by late summer there'd be tomatoes every meal. Alan remembered being here as a kid and sitting down to a meal of sliced tomatoes and rhubarb pie and not knowing which he was supposed to eat first.

Uncle Ross was still upstairs. Alice had cooked a chicken, and the mashed potatoes to go with it, and Jon had brought a plastic bag of bread to the table from the top of the fridge, though no butter or knife.

"White supper," Jon announced when the chicken, bread, and potatoes were in the centre of the table. Alice threw him a look to see if he was complaining or just being arty. The backs of Jon's hands were still dirty from wrestling the boat. Alan had ended up scraping all the algae gunk off the hull while Jon was off having what he said was an important talk with his mother.

They ate for a while without speaking, not an uncomfortable silence but in a kind Alan didn't like for the way it made sounds stand out, forks on plates, and chewing. He hated the liquid sounds of his relatives chewing.

He eyed an empty water glass at the sink. Was it the same glass? Had she just dumped it there?

"Who's that guy?" Jon asked his mother, nodding at the beaded musician on the cover of the magazine she was still reading, propped beside her plate.

"Another millionaire." Alice didn't look at her son but took a solid gulp of wine to punctuate how she felt about this.

For a while Alice and Jon had opinions about the toughness of the chicken, and about the butcher for selling it to them, and then Alan wondered aloud about the state of Uncle Ross. Alice joked that he was by now either asleep or dead.

They fell silent again, then heard a loud thump from above, from Ross's room. Pleased with the timing, Alice said, "Well, I guess not."

Alan sat still, staring alertly into his plate, wondering who was going to go up. It would be insulting if he made the first move. He took another bite of chicken, which was only dry and not the fault of any butcher. He couldn't suggest that someone go investigate, for wouldn't that be implying that they didn't care? Or he could joke about taking Ross up some tough old chicken, but they'd see through that one.

No one moved. This was stuff you couldn't talk about, not

in a million years.

Alan thrilled suddenly with the notion—the back of his neck actually tingled—that, upstairs, death might be happening and no one here was going to budge because of it.

He glanced at his cousin and his aunt. They weren't going anywhere. But he saw now that his own urge to check on his uncle wasn't overwhelming. The thump hadn't been as loud as a man falling, for one thing. Nowhere as loud as that.

Eventually Jon said into his plate, "So how's highrise life?" Before Alan could swallow enough food to answer, Jon asked something else. "How's the feeder? Ever get her up?"

"Yeah. Last spring."

From inside her magazine Alice snorted, repeating to herself, "Ever get 'er up."

Alan didn't want to go into this. The hummingbird feeder had been Jon's Christmas gift to him. He'd unwrapped it to find dirt smudges and residue of red syrup inside. Its being a castoff apparently didn't faze Jon, who was pressing now with that interest gift-givers have.

"Yeah. Last spring."

"Hummers come round?"

"Sure."

"Many?"

"I think—I dunno...."

"What?"

"I think I might have killed them."

Alice pulled her head out of her magazine for this.

Alan gave them the brief version. He'd read in *Harrowsmith* how you could make your own hummingbird food—sugar, water, red dye. But he'd figured the dye couldn't be good for them, nor could white sugar, so he'd customized by getting some demerara sugar at a health food store. Demerara had to be better, it had to have more food in it than white. It took a while for the hummingbirds to come, but then they did, lots of them, it was great watching the little vibrating bullets of life, some of them sequinned, red and green, some dull but magically vital nonetheless, unthinkable hearts going a hundred beats a second. They came for a week and then, suddenly, none.

"I went back and read the rest of the article," Alan smirked, despite himself, "and read that basically anything except that stupid recipe is poisonous to them. Anything: honey, molasses.... So—"

"So you go granola and kill them!" Alice shrieked with delight. "Bonny-boy! This is good, this is good. You gotta admit, this is perfect. He wipes out a whole region!"

"Any come back?" Jon asked, not laughing. It was hard to hear him over his mother's hoots and noises.

"Drained it. Haven't tried it since."

"I'm sorry," Alice caught her breath, wiping her eyes with the back of her hand, "but really, it's perfect. It's the irony of do-gooders, it really is. Bonny-boy, I'm sorry, but you're a do-gooder."

"Well, I mean, how could anyone possibly think white sugar could possibly be—?"

Alice interrupted with a tilt of the head, a raising of eyebrows. "Bonny-boy, don't sweat it. I love your mistakes." She looked at him almost warmly. "Only angels can kill hummingbirds, eh?" She took a good sip and added, as if serious, as if to explain, "Only angels can catch 'em." Then cackled falsely, and now Alan could see the rough edge to her, the odd, excited shaking. She was different tonight, a nervousness.

From somewhere in that nervousness, Alice suddenly turned to her son and asked him, "When's the last time you saw Daddy smile, Jon-love?"

Alan was unprepared for such a question, so corny and foreign at this table. He felt embarrassed for them both. But his cousin appeared to be thinking, searching his memory.

"How 'bout you, Bonny-boy?" she asked Alan.

She seemed perfectly sincere, and her eyes were warm. So Alan placed Uncle Ross's face in various situations and tried to remember a smile. For the life of him he couldn't. He recalled the time some years back when Jon had fallen into the stream and then stayed in swimming and ruined everything in his wallet, but Ross's laughter at the sight of the wallet had come out of a face that showed teeth like a snarl. But there must have been a time.

Jon shook his head, he couldn't remember either. His mother nodded, letting her gaze fall gently onto the table.

Full, Alan leaned back in his chair. He stared up at the ceiling, as if trying to see into Uncle Ross's room.

Alice sobbed. It might have been a laugh, but it sounded like a sob. By the time Alan looked at her, her face showed nothing, but he saw Jon considering his mother hard as well.

Looking as though he'd decided something, Jon put down

his chicken leg in a way that was almost elegant. He kept his eyes on his mother. For the first time since Alan had known him, Jon seemed complicated, almost wise. And, trading a deep stare with her son, Alice looked to be in some kind of agreement with him. Staring like that into her son's eyes, she sobbed again.

Not knowing quite why, Alan grew frightened.

"Daphne should be here tonight," Aunt Alice said softly, and her eyes went up to the ceiling, looking through it. Jon had nothing to say to this, and Alan didn't dare, for it was beginning to dawn on him what was going on.

"But you are." Alice turned to Alan. Her voice fell almost to baby-talk. "You're here, Bonny-boy. You're family as much as anyone."

This time thrill crackled through and his hair stood up for real. He pictured Ross up on the bed, one foot still on the floor after one last, desperate, weak, stomp.

Alice and Jon were both staring quietly at him. They wanted him to know, and now he did. He saw how they'd all simply been waiting. It had been years and years, everyone waiting for this night.

GOD'S PRICKS

.

It was early spring, and evenings the cold came on so quickly and seriously it made you think about survival. At the firepit Sam felt an urgency going on all fours to blow into the damp kindling. Life can get simple.

"So—so what's this all about?" Michael pointed his finger at Sam, then at himself, then waggled it at the campsite and the growing fire. They had just sat down, breathing from the work.

"What's what all about?" Though Sam knew. He just wasn't used to this new Michael, this raising of real questions.

"Us here together. What does it mean?"

"Maybe it's just good to get away. Relax."

At this, Michael leaned at Sam to peer admonishment over the tops of his glasses, his face flickering orange and cut with shadows. They had done little but set up, swat bugs, attempt to cook inappropriate food after scouring the dripping woods for stuff to burn, two middle-aged bozos who hadn't come prepared. And Sam so on edge, hating it whenever Michael cried and dreading the time when Michael might want to talk about his agony.

"Relax?" Michael lifted an eyebrow, its irony lit up orange.

Besides Michael's obvious sadness he'd had a gin-soaked look—the puffiness, and in the eyes a skewed clarity that bulged out of red rims. Sam didn't know if Michael had been drinking, but so what if he had. When someone's child dies you naturally, even aggressively, forgive them everything. And anyway Sam lived in a glass house when it came to drinking.

It wasn't out of forgiveness that he had agreed to the camping trip. It was more that they'd once been good friends, and maybe still were, despite Michael stealing from him. You couldn't beat high school friendships, you really couldn't. Here they were bumping into each other in a bar neither of them frequented, the years melting away under the light of simple eye contact. Heads slowly shaken at the immensity of all that had happened, not just to Michael but to Sam and to everyone. So they got a bit drunk and decided to take off camping. The next morning Sam was fuzzy as to the planning except that it was to be a simple operation. It had to do with getting out of the city. Eating beans out of a can, seeing stars at night. Sam remembered thinking that maybe he could help his old friend out. A daughter dying, and Sally leaving. The second one he knew about.

Michael picked him up at his apartment, Sam standing smiling in the door hoisting a sleeping-bag in one hand and a pillow in the other, that's all, a kind of joke. Out on the highway they couldn't help but notice they were headed for a horizon of nothing but raincloud. They kept driving, neither mentioning it, and this made any weather puny.

Michael's scenario was this: Sally had kept up appearances for their sick daughter's sake, then when Jennifer finally died Sally too left him for good, Michael's double whammy. Sam figured you couldn't have your slate wiped much cleaner. But reading Michael's face here in the car he recalculated. Michael's slate was looking full as hell. Under the surface a sour panic, a sick animal in a bag. You didn't want to watch Michael's face for long.

They hardly spoke on the two-hour drive to The Cliff, a campsite known from long before, from their grad debauch, in fact— a stupid place to go because a cliff was what it was, a clearing in the trees bordered on one side by a thirty-foot drop to the river rocks. Sam assumed they'd agreed on this spot as a further tip of the hat to the past. A time before care. A time when he, not Michael, was with Sally, and he and Michael were still friends. Because the other part of the scenario was that, back around then, Michael had taken Sally from him. You could construe it that she had left of her own accord, but in truth Michael had taken her. Of all of them he was the best looking. His silences proved not to be shyness but precocious reserve. He'd managed to hang onto the "Michael" in the face of guys' continual attempts at "Mike", and this seemed to affect the girls in ways the guys could only dimly comprehend. Even back then he'd had a handle on charm, knew where the trigger was. So he'd had choice, and he'd chosen Sally.

They arrived, sat silently a moment gazing through the windshield bugs at where they were, then climbed out to stretch. The campsite was dark, trees dense on three sides. The car ticked behind them. Sam recalled almost nothing of the place save this feeling in his stomach at the thought of going drunkenly over that edge. A bluejay landed on a branch hanging over the drop and it screamed, a wretched sound out of something pretty. The bugs found them. Michael laughed as he swatted at his neck, and he said almost affectionately, glancing back at Sam, "God's little pricks."

Sam cracked a beer and watched him unfurl the tent, then squat with a big muddy stone to bang pegs into the hard ground, grunting involuntarily, looking pure. No Sally, no daughter. Other than the greying hair it could have been Michael twenty years ago.

The first night was fine, a relief to in fact escape something—call it the city, or call it another morning you don't necessarily want to em-brace. There being no chairs in the tent they sat in the car, sipping Irish whiskey, waiting out the rain. Whiskey was dangerous for him but probably not, he told himself, as dangerous as life was for Michael. They turned the radio on and the night began to pass. Sam decided it wasn't degraded, this drinking in a parked car—they were sitting, they were comfortable, it could have been a living-room.

Michael didn't bring it up. Once he cried, quietly, and an-other time he gasped, out of the blue. He had to take deep breaths to calm himself. Occasionally he shook his head and said, "I don't know...," or "Man, what can you say...." but otherwise he talked about baseball. How good Montreal was despite no big payroll. In the ma-jors a few Canadians —Walker, Stairs, Dickson—were having huge years. Stairs and Dickson were from New Brunswick. Michael re-minded him how, the year before, Stairs had tied a major-league record for RBIs in an inning, and added quietly, staring out the windshield at the blackness of nothing, that if Stairs was American or from Toronto he'd be doing TV commercials because of it.

At this Michael smiled and said, "We're so proud, we don't

brag."

Sam was about to toss in a joke that New Brunswickers were too ugly for TV but he didn't, because Michael was anything but ugly and it might have made him self-conscious, uncomfortable for Sam's sake.

In the morning he rattled his bottle of aspirin at Michael while gulping some down with a beer. Michael said he didn't take aspirin any more.

"Hey," he added with a little laugh, getting Sam to look at him. "A hangover's nothing. A hangover makes sense. Hangover's a fucking relief."

Sam wasn't of this opinion at all, and it must have been the expression on his face that made Michael laugh, kindly.

In the bar they'd heard reports about Jennifer's battle all along, rumours of it having spread to the bone, someone else saying the brain, in any case horrified gossip that caused long silences. Bald half her life, a final year of bed and sledgehammer medicine, Jennifer made it to nine. Their only child. For all intents and purposes Sally had been with Craig Fennel for two years already and of course she took flak for this, as if in light of Jennifer she was heartless and more at fault than others whose marriages had broken. People had to point their emotions somewhere, though clear thinking led you to see that blame couldn't possibly enter into this one—unless you wanted to aim it at some notion of God or the principle of your choice, whatever it was that brought you here to suffer and die while keeping mum with its secrets, if there were any. Leaving you hunched over the table under the big-screen game, mute and staring off at the story of Michael and Jennifer and Sally, feeling too present, yet hardly hearing the machine-glorious beeps of video poker games, somebody yelling because they've won three or four dollars.

The path was steep and he was grateful someone had sprayed the root footholds fluorescent orange. At the bottom, stepping rock to rock, he followed Michael up the riverbed. A slight breeze cut up the valley and into their faces, so the bugs weren't bad. They had to speak over the rushing water-noise.

"Another thing we forgot—rods."

"Seeing them's okay," Michael said, not turning around to talk to him. "I'd rather just see them anyway."

It being cloudy Michael had the idea of trying to find and watch some trout, because when it was sunny the water surface reflected too much and you couldn't. Sam could vaguely recall seeing a large trout in a stream like this once, fleeing through clear water, its big lidless eye taking him in.

"Okay, careful," Michael turned and whispered, fifty feet from the pool. "Don't jiggle any rocks. Step only on big—" Turning back around he missed his footing, tried to compensate and fell backwards. Sam broke most of his fall but Michael ended up sitting in a pool of icy water.

"AHHH! SHIT! WOOOOOO!"

Laughing, shouting, he scrambled up quickly. Sam had him by the arm.

"Perfect, wooooo!" Michael was talking fast from the cold water. "Perfect—I tell *you* to be careful, down I go. Thank you." He was looking at the rocks, nodding to them. "Thank you. Thanks for the reminder." He's serious. Or, at least, not sarcastic.

He said nothing important all that day, though he cried from time to time. His crying had almost taken on a casualness. He'd go still, perhaps remembering something. His head would dip, his shoulders rounding, a small collapsing into himself. His face would contort and his hand come up to cradle his forehead. He'd suffer the spasm, his shoulders going up and down, not much noise escaping. And that would be that. He would pick up his head and wipe his eyes. With no embarrassment he'd continue their conversation, even if it was about something as small as baseball or trout.

Sitting on his log ten feet away, Michael pointed at him. "You've got a dead bug or something on your forehead. Driving me nuts."

Sam swiped at his head with the back of his hand.

"Still there." Michael brushed at his own head to show him.

Sam swiped at his head harder.

"Jesus. *Here*." Michael laughed as he strode up. He put his face a foot from Sam's, perfectly still, breathing delicately through his nose as he pinched at the stuck thing, his concentration unnerving because it was like he was staring Sam right in the eyes.

"I couldn't take anything you've been saying seriously, this thing squished on your head."

Michael had sipped a few calm beer, not drinking as much as he had the night before, and Sam was aware of being watched tucking into the whiskey. He wondered what the rumours were about him, what conclusions had been drawn regarding his marriages and alcohol. He wondered if Sally's name ever came up as part of the equation. Because it should. Some night he would love to arrive unnoticed at the table of gossipers and announce simply and with a shrug: It's always been her.

Laughing, they discovered that the immense, manly steaks they'd bought on the way out of town were only out of consideration for each other. Beef didn't sit well with Sam, made him tired and, according to his last wife, angry. Michael said he'd been sick of steak for twenty years. And these were so thick they demanded extra forays into the woods for more soggy deadfall to stuff into the embers and try to coax alive. Their frying pan could hold only one at a time. Close to midnight, when the first steak was almost done, they frisbeed the other raw off the cliff and into the river, a treasure for downstream raccoons and other carnal whatnots.

They did get into the one steak pretty good. They had no knife and passed it dripping and lukewarm on a fork, tearing bites out of it, really having to use teeth. Juice all over their chins and cheeks. After a couple of passes Michael got angry at this, mostly due to Sam's having drunkenly dropped it in the dirt. Chewing and grinning, Sam watched Michael rinse the meat with half a beer, then rinse the axe and a plank with the other half. By now Michael was a bit drunk also. In any case his humour was back. When he readied the axe he growled softly for Sam's benefit, then made the appropriate noise hacking the meat in two.

Waking up in the morning—actually it was noon—he did go aspirinless, but only for several minutes, and this because they were out of anything, even alcohol, to drink. He had to get himself down to the river, almost fainting with pain and the hell of standing, the hell of being awake at all. Sometimes in the unbearable clarity of it all you just want to sink to the linoleum or dirt and yell as loud as you had to, scrape your face into the bottommost grit and let the noises come out.

But soon he was belly-down on the rocks, sucking water from his cupped hand, his ass still hurting from when he'd fallen and slid. He was wearing only the underwear and T-shirt he'd slept in.

He noticed a shadow, then feet. Michael standing over him.

"If the goal—I'm not saying it is—but if the goal is to be really alive and alert, then *mistakes* are the best tools for helping us do it."

Sam was having trouble and the droning, rehearsed quality of Michael's voice was hard. He felt close to gagging. He'd had too much cold water too fast. Rubbing icy water into his face, he could smell last night's meat on his hands. Water was beading up on them, on the grease. Michael was talking again.

"I mean think about it. If everything's cruising along fine would you ever look at yourself?"

"...You wouldn't, no...."

"Anything so-called 'bad', like you bang your knee on a chair, whatever, is good. Because it wakes you up. Even, even something like Jennifer."

Sam twisted awkwardly to look up at him, to acknowledge this. Here it was at last. He put a hand up to shield his eyes from Michael's face as if it were the sun.

"I mean, there's, there's no lid on the jar we're in. You know? It's the one, it's the one positive I've come up with. In what's happened." Michael smiled and Sam could see it was for his sake. "It reminds you you're alive. Makes life vivid. It's like you've hit the banana peel and you're mid-air and more awake than you ever wanted to be."

Sam was trying hard not to retch.

"Everything's pretty bright. And it all fits."

Sam moaned softly in a way he hoped sounded appropriate. About to start the beginning of getting up, he saw Michael tense, and plant his feet.

"Even, even this." His face quickly clenched so tight it went white over his cheek bones and nose, Michael slapped his hands together, a tremendous painful *whock* that echoed up and down the small river valley. He did it six or seven times, Sam watching paralysed from below.

Sam slept as long as he could. They got things packed by mid-afternoon, Michael not caring that the tent was heaved into his trunk muddy like that. The garbage and bottles were a problem for they had no bags. The beer cases had turned to mush. Sam hated it, pinching up smelly blood-dripping cellophane from the ground to place into the trunk where Michael pointed, in the tent's folds.

The muck and labour seemed to fit the futility of their camping trip in general. Sally's name had not come up, not even as a conciliatory joke, an acknowledging of what they shared. Which made him wonder—Jesus, the look of the crumpled beer cans in the fire pit gave him a headache—made him wonder if Michael did in fact know they shared her. Her touch. The look in her eyes. Sure, Sam and Sally hadn't been more than eighteen, and Michael had gone through a marriage and child with her, but still.

With Michael taking a last hike down to the river, Sam took some trash off into the trees. Garbage like this was only eye pollution and if you hid it it was not even that. As he re-entered the clearing a jay screamed at him from the other side, but he would not entertain that kind of cheap coincidence. Nor did he entertain the thought that had just dawned, that he and Sally might have nothing heartfelt to say to each other any more, aside from the obvious and the sad.

Michael drove so slowly it irritated Sam more and more. Though he'd arrived at and understood the hard fact that the only real reason he had for getting back was perhaps a shower. But when Michael took a detour to an old dump to maybe see bears, Sam sensed conspiracy. They sat overlong, saw no bears, and on the crawling drive back to the highway, Michael asked a question and the conspiracy was proven.

"So, gonna give it a try?"

"...Try?"

"You know. Hootch." Michael brought a fist up and swigged from the thumb.

Sam dimly remembered last night, them talking about his drinking. He'd admitted to "what might be called a problem". He'd even exaggerated things for drama. Big declaration of cleaning up his act, starting over, all the clichés. Right now the whole notion felt frail, wispy, like fantasy, and the thought of actually doing it, awful.

"Sure. I think maybe I will."

Thankfully Michael said nothing more. They pulled out of the leafy dirt road and back onto the highway, everything speeding up, pointing in the right direction, feeling better. It would make sense to Michael that everyone should be on a self-improvement kick. But it occurred to Sam now that something between him and Michael had shifted. Something ominous, and almost articulated. In retrospect the whole weekend took a turn. Sally's name had not come up and Jennifer's only the once and Sam hadn't helped. But had any of that ever been on the agenda at all? Was it possible that, if this weekend had anything to do with someone being helped, that someone wasn't Michael?

He looked across at his old friend, whom he no longer knew. Michael's hands easy on the wheel, a light control. His face looked engaged with shit, and with more shit to come, but not worried. Ready. A boxer in a ring. He didn't look worried at all. Sam could picture Michael with no lid on the jar he was sitting in.

"Ever seen the swifts?"

It was almost as if Michael had read his mind. Sam had been doing nicely, and then in the very first fit of savouring a drink, trying to picture what he had on hand at home, Michael asked this question and then turned off the highway, near Oromocto. A sign had said Old Mill, beside which was a simplistic, white portrait of a bird, a government rendition of a chimney swift. Now they were travelling down a side road in the wrong direction, heading away from the cold beer in the back of his fridge.

Sam shook his head. No he hadn't ever seen the fucking swifts.

"It's perfect timing. Sundown's when they do it."

Ten miles later they were parked near an immense pile of terracotta rubble out of which rose a massive brick chimney, perhaps sixty feet tall. It was like a bombed Dresden factory, but alone and surrounded by New Brunswick bush. Two other cars were there, out-of-province cars. An older couple in tourist whites stood respectfully staring up, the man holding binoculars at the ready, elbows cocked. The other couple was younger and the man talked excitedly, explaining everything to his wife as he pointed up at the swirl of birds, the hundreds, thousands of them, describing with his arm the immense whirlpool they were making, as if she couldn't see it for herself.

Sam found the birds hard to look at. Maybe it was the bright light backing them. And they were loud, a thousand pipings at once, their noise a solid yet needling thing. They formed a funnel not unlike a child's drawing of a tornado, the bottom tip flirting with the chimney top. The birds nearer the bottom swirled faster, or seemed to, as their circle was smaller. A minute would pass and a string of ten or twenty of them suddenly would drop into the chimney and not come out.

"Look at the little pricks." Michael was smiling non-stop and fondly, as though the birds were doing this for their entertainment.

Sam found them dizzying, disturbing. He wondered how long Michael would make him stay. He glanced at the old woman, who'd been watching him back. He knew what he must look like and she made him feel filthy and ashamed.

Michael's loud laugh made him look up. Both of the other couples were shouting. The swifts were doing it. Their huge sky-filling corkscrew was falling, they were going in *en masse*.

Sam gasped and went back on his heels. It was as if the thousands of birds were being vacuumed from below, being taken helplessly by earth's dirty pipe. He might faint, this awful noiseless sucking in of thousands of birds, this draining of the sky. Michael stood beside him erect and eager and his laughing was low, almost a growl, as if challenging the world to keep it going, to turn itself inside out after the birds were gone.